"I don't understand... Are you saying you want to marry me?"

He didn't roll his eyes. He didn't have to. Instead, shaking his head, he laughed. Not the nice, warm kind of laughter that accompanied an amusing joke, but the humorless sort that people did when something wasn't funny.

Just wildly implausible to the point of being ludicrous.

Her fingers bit into the folder as she felt his laughter ripple through her.

"No, I don't want to marry you, Effie."

He shifted against the sofa, one muscular arm lifting to rest it along the back of the cushions. "But don't take it personally. I don't want to marry anyone. I do, however, *need* a wife."

Now he was making even less sense.

"*Need* is a strong word, Mr. Kane," she said slowly. It was actually an odd word. The only man she knew of who *needed* a wife was St. John Rivers and he was a fictional missionary.

"Achileas," he corrected her again. "And maybe you're right. Need *is* too strong a word. Perhaps it would be more accurate to say that I *require* a wife."

Louise Fuller was a tomboy who hated pink and always wanted to be the prince—not the princess! Now she enjoys creating heroines who aren't pretty pushovers but are strong, believable women. Before writing for Harlequin, she studied literature and philosophy at university, then worked as a reporter on her local newspaper. She lives in Royal Tunbridge Wells with her impossibly handsome husband, Patrick, and their six children.

Books by Louise Fuller

Harlequin Presents

The Rules of His Baby Bargain
The Man She Should Have Married
Italian's Scandalous Marriage Plan
Beauty in the Billionaire's Bed
The Italian's Runaway Cinderella

Christmas with a Billionaire

The Christmas She Married the Playboy

The Sicilian Marriage Pact

The Terms of the Sicilian's Marriage

Visit the Author Profile page
at Harlequin.com for more titles.

Louise Fuller

MAID FOR THE GREEK'S RING

HARLEQUIN
PRESENTS

ISBN-13: 978-1-335-58363-5

Maid for the Greek's Ring

Copyright © 2022 by Louise Fuller

Harlequin Enterprises ULC
22 Adelaide St. West, 41st Floor
Toronto, Ontario M5H 4E3, Canada
www.Harlequin.com

Printed in U.S.A.

MAID FOR THE GREEK'S RING

CHAPTER ONE

THE HONEYMOON SUITE at the legendary Stanmore Hotel in London's Mayfair was quite possibly the most beautiful room Effie Price had ever seen. It was certainly one of the most expensive, although not as expensive as the Royal Suite upstairs, where one night alone would cost more than half her annual salary.

As a maid.

She glanced down at her neat black uniform dress and white apron. And right now, she was being paid to clean the room, not gawp at it.

But it was hard not to just stand and admire the cream-coloured living room. It was big enough to land a small plane in, and as well as the glittering chandeliers and bespoke handcrafted furniture the suite was a technophile's dream, with remote-controlled everything.

Was it worth it?

Running her hand across the marble swags on the feature fireplace, she sighed. It was a rhetorical question. Aside from not having the money, she was twenty-two years old and had never had a boyfriend. This might be the closest she was ever going to get to a honeymoon suite.

'There you are. I've been looking for you—'

Picking up a pile of used towels, Effie glanced over her shoulder as Janine and Emily, her friends and fellow chambermaids, put their heads round the door. Actually, according to her job description, they were 'accommodation assistants', but nobody except management ever referred to any of them as anything but maids.

Reaching out, Janine grabbed the pile of towels and dumped them firmly in the laundry basket. 'Shoo!' She pointed at the door. 'We can finish up.'

Effie shook her head. 'It's okay. I'm nearly done.'

Mentally she ticked off her to-do list.

In the bedroom, the Icelandic down duvet sat plumply on the Christian Liaigre four-poster bed, with the pillowcase folds facing away from the door so the guests didn't see them when they walked in. All the woodwork was buffed, the mini bar and desk were both restocked, the bath and sink had been cleaned, toiletries replenished, towels and robes replaced, mirrors polished—

'I just need to vacuum.'

'I can do that.' Eyes narrowing, Emily jerked the handle of the vacuum out of reach. 'Come on, Effie. We've got this. You have somewhere to be, remember? This is the big day.'

Effie felt her stomach flip over. *The big day.*

It sounded like one of those essay-writing prompts you got at school. She breathed out unsteadily. She had loved making up stories in her head, but her dyslexia had made writing them down so hard. Often, she'd chosen to use words she could spell rather than embarrass herself.

Only this big day was not in her head. It was happening in just over an hour.

A wave of part panic, part excitement crested inside her. Ever since she was a little girl, she had dreamed about owning her own perfumery business. Her mother, Sam, had worked from home as a beautician, and every day women would arrive to have a facial or their make-up done. To Effie, watching the lines around their eyes soften, it had seemed to her almost as if her mother was weaving a spell.

And, for her, making perfume had that same transformative magic. Not just the process of turning the raw ingredients into a unique scent, but the alchemy that scent performed on the person wearing it. The people smelling it. Perfume could change your mood…make you feel happy or sexy or strong.

But she didn't just want to change the lives of strangers. She wanted to get her mother out of a situation where she had to constantly worry about money.

Today, finally, she would be able to make that happen.

She felt her skin prickle with nerves and excitement. She still couldn't quite believe it, but if this meeting went well, and the bank agreed to the loan, the money would be in her account in forty-eight hours. And then her life would change too. Finally, she would stop living in a minor key.

That was her dream—her promise to herself.

And if she kept that promise then all of this—emptying bins, picking up other people's dirty laundry—would be over. She looked over at her friends, her throat tightening. There were some plus points to her job, though.

Two minutes later she was making her way along the corridor.

Her glasses were hurting a little, and she had just slipped them off and was rubbing the place on her face where they had made a small indentation when a man stepped out of the lift, a woman tottering beside him, clutching his arm as if it were a lifebelt. Her footsteps faltered. The guests in this part of the hotel were either wealthy, famous, or wealthy *and* famous, but either way eye contact and conversation were discouraged and, lowering her gaze, she edged closer to the wall as she walked.

'This doesn't look right.'

The man's voice made her head jerk up. More than that: it made goosebumps break out on her arms.

She didn't usually notice voices, mainly because she experienced the world through other senses—how things smelled and tasted. But this man's voice was impossible to ignore. It was rich and deep, with a teasing, shifting accent.

If it was a scent, she thought, it would be a mix of lavender and sun-warmed tobacco, with just a hint of tonka bean.

Make that burnt caramel, she thought, as her eyes fluttered upwards to his face and took in thick, dark hair that gleamed like polished jet beneath the recessed downlights. Sculpted bones beneath smooth gold skin. A dangerous, curving mouth and blue eyes—the bluest eyes she had ever seen. Blue eyes she wanted to high-dive into.

Even though in reality she couldn't actually swim.

He was the most astonishingly, conspicuously beautiful man she had ever seen.

Her throat felt dry and tight, and suddenly it was difficult to catch her breath. She reached out, touching the wall to steady herself. It was that or fall over.

The man was looking down at the woman beside him, and for that she couldn't blame him.

Whoever she was, she was his equal in beauty. All long limbs and a mane of glossy blonde hair. Like the horses her father used to watch on the television, walking around the paddock before the race started.

The memory pounded through her like their thundering hooves and suddenly she was shaking inside. She didn't want to think about her father. Thinking about him would just make her feel crushed and powerless, and right now she needed to be strong. Or at least to appear strong.

Only that was hard to do if, like her, you were small and ordinary. And forgettable.

'This is the wrong floor.'

The man stepped backwards, pulling the woman into the lift with him. Turning to hit the button, his eyes met Effie's and she blinked as his blue gaze slammed into hers with the force of a wave.

She felt her feet slide sideways. Around her the walls shuddered and fell and everything she knew or thought she knew was swept away. She was standing in a place she didn't recognise, her body quivering with a wild, dizzying, nameless yearning for—

The lift doors closed.

For what?

Slipping her glasses back on, she stared at her reflection in the polished steel doors, panic and confusion banging inside her. She had no idea how to answer that question. How could she? She had nothing to compare the feeling to.

Not that she minded being a virgin. In fact, when her friends wept over their latest break-up she felt relieved. Her parents' unhappy, lopsided marriage had made her nervous about trusting in big things like love and devotion. As for sex— she simply hadn't met the right person.

Or even the wrong one.

It wasn't just that she was quiet and reserved. Being her mother's carer had meant there was little opportunity for a normal teenage social life. Sex, intimacy and relationships had by-passed her completely, so that aside from a few clumsy kisses on New Year's Eve she had never touched a man or been touched. And this man— this stranger—hadn't touched her, only his gaze had felt like a touch. It had felt real, *intimate*.

Shaking her head, Effie backed away from the lift and hurried along the corridor.

It made no sense. *She* was making no sense. Obviously she was nervous about the meeting. That was why her head was spinning. And why her body felt taut and jittery.

On the ground floor, she checked her watch. She had left plenty of time to get changed, but as usual when she walked through the main part of the hotel in her uniform several people stopped her to ask for directions to the restaurant or the lift and it took another twenty minutes before she finally got downstairs.

She needed to get a move on. Sidestepping the clusters of guests, she headed towards one of the side entrances, undoing her apron as she walked and pulling her hair out of its bun into a ponytail.

It was too late to get changed now, although it didn't really matter. The bank knew what she did and she wasn't ashamed of her job. But there were still some people who couldn't see past the uniform, and she didn't want to be defined by any prejudice that might provoke.

Her pulse twitched.

What would be wonderful would be to look like the woman from the lift. Smooth and glossily sophisticated. Instead, she was thin, with boring brown hair and boring brown eyes beneath boring brown-rimmed glasses.

But maybe if she'd been smooth and sophisticated, she would have been too enchanted by her own appearance to think about making perfume. And she loved making perfume. For her, scent was so much more than just a finishing touch to an outfit. It was a ticket to a life far beyond the four walls of her tiny bedsit.

She felt a rush of excitement as exhilarating and potent as any of the perfumes she created, and a faint smile pulled at her mouth as she stepped into the bright spring morning. She

should definitely add that into her proposal.
Maybe she should just put a note on her phone—

Her phone!

She stumbled forward, her foot catching on
the thought as if it was a crack in the pavement
and, yanking open her bag, fumbled inside.
But her phone wasn't there. It was sitting in her
locker. Without it she would never be able to find
her way to the bank. She had no sense of direction, and it was a waste of time asking people
for help in London. They almost always turned
out to be tourists.

She was just going to have to go back and
get it.

Spinning round, she began swiftly retracing
her steps, her skin prickling with anxiety.

It would be all right, she told herself. It was
only two stops on the underground plus a short
walk, and she still had twenty minutes until her
appointment.

She hurried down the street to the side en-
trance of the hotel, jumping out of her skin as a
huge black SUV glided past her noiselessly and
slid to a stop beside the kerb. It would be okay.
All she had to do was go to her locker—

The door to the hotel swung open and a man
erupted into the daylight, flanked by two heavily built men in black suits. His eyes were hidden
behind a pair of sleek sunglasses, his attention

fixed on the phone in his hand. But she didn't need to see them to know they were blue.

It was the man from the lift, and he was heading straight for her.

For a few half-seconds she hesitated, one foot hovering above the step, her brain telling her to move, her body frozen. Finally, she made a last-minute attempt to sidestep him, but it was too late. She had a fleeting impression of a broad, masculine chest in a blue shirt, topped by a dark-stubbled scowl, and then her bag tumbled from her shoulder and she let out a gasp as her body collided with a solid wall of muscle.

'Oh, I'm so sorry!' she apologised automatically—guests were always right. But her words were cut off as the man from the lift reached out and caught her elbow to steady them both. His grip didn't hurt, but his beauty did. Her heartbeat stumbled. Up close, his face was arresting, extraordinary. But it wasn't just his face making her head feel light.

Beneath that impeccable dark suit there was a barely concealed animal vitality, a power and a ferocity that filled her with a prickling kind of panic, so that she was suddenly and acutely conscious of the rise and fall of her breath beneath her too-tight skin.

'You wouldn't need to be sorry if you'd been looking where you're going,' he said curtly, staring down at her in a way that made her body feel taut and loose at the same time. He took a step closer and tapped the lens of her glasses. 'Maybe these need replacing.'

Effie stared up at him, her cheeks colouring— not just at the injustice of his remark but at the intimacy of his action.

She slipped her arm free. 'Actually, you walked into me, Mr…' She hesitated, waiting for him to provide his name.

'Kane,' he said finally. 'Achileas Kane.'

The name hovered between them like one of the glittering dragonflies she sometimes saw by the Serpentine when she went to Hyde Park after work. She shivered inside. Achileas…from Achilles, the greatest warrior of Ancient Greece, legendary hero of Troy. Formidable. Ruthless. Remorseless.

And the current occupant of the Stanmore Hotel's Royal Suite.

'And you are…?'

His voice was soft, but there was a hard undercurrent in it that made her shake inside.

'Effie Price.' Feeling the shimmering, dismissive never-heard-of-you sweep of his blue gaze, she said quickly, 'And, like I was saying, you walked into me, Mr Kane. So maybe I'm not the only one who needs glasses.'

She felt her breath catch, and something stirred inside her as his pupils flared like twin lighthouse beams across a darkening sea. Behind her the noise from the main road seemed to fade and she was aware of nothing beyond the beating of her heart.

Skin prickling, needing to escape from his penetrating blue gaze, she reached down to pick up her bag. But he beat her to it, and as they straightened up he held it just out of her grasp. Stray beams of sunlight added tiger stripes to the mitred planes of his mesmerising face.

'Is that right?' he said smoothly.

She felt a rush of irritation. The sun might seek him out, burnishing him with celestial golden light like a mythical hero, but nothing could gild his arrogance.

'Yes, it is. Oh, and while we're on the subject I'm taking back my apology,' she added, when she could breathe again. Just because he looked like a Greek god, didn't mean he could act like one. Throwing down thunderbolts with his eyes and looming over her in his dark suit so that he took over the entire world—or at least the bit she was standing in.

'Excuse me?'

Now he was looking at her as if seeing her for the first time.

Probably he was. She had spent most of her life being ignored and side-lined—why should this moment be any different? Or perhaps he was just stunned that anyone, particularly someone like her, should question his world view.

'Taking it back?' His voice had dropped another notch, but it was his mouth that caught her attention, curling up at the corner into a sensual question mark that seemed to tug her upwards like a fish on a hook.

Suddenly, instead of feeling side-lined, she felt sideswiped by the fierce intensity of his focus, but she just about managed to hold his gaze. 'I'm not sorry,' she said shakily. 'How can I be sorry for something I didn't do? I was just being polite,' she said quickly, answering her own question as his eyes narrowed on her face. 'In fact, you should be apologising to me.'

Seriously?

Achileas Kane gazed down at the woman tapping one small foot in front of him, his fury vying with wordless disbelief.

To say that he was in a bad mood would be something of an understatement. The day had started on a wrong note when they had finally left the party at Nico's house this morning.

They. His jaw tightened. He hadn't arrived with Tamara, and he certainly hadn't been planning on leaving with her. Their nine-week relationship had been a purely physical and mutually satisfying affair that he had brought to a close a good six months ago.

But for some reason last night Tamara had decided that, far from being over, their relationship needed rekindling, and on a more serious footing. She'd got horribly drunk and then been horribly sick. Afterwards she'd refused to let go of his arm, clinging on to him as tenaciously as the ivy on Nico's Georgian mansion, so that in the end it had been easier just to bring her back to his hotel room and let her sleep it off.

Only when he'd told her he was leaving she'd gone nuclear, screaming abuse not just in English but Russian too, and threatening him with all manner of violent and painful acts of retribution.

And when that had failed to change his mind, she'd told him she was going to call her father.

Oleg Ivanov was a Russian oligarch. Immensely wealthy in his own right, he had recently married off one daughter to a tech billionaire and was now actively looking for suitable grooms for her two younger sisters.

Achileas's spine tensed. And he was going to have to keep on looking. Matrimony was not on his agenda and, given that one in two marriages ended in divorce, he wasn't exactly sure why it was on anyone else's.

You could make countless vows in front of an endless stream of witnesses and it wouldn't change the facts. Fidelity was a social construct, not a biological imperative, and as the unwanted, unacknowledged bastard son of shipping tycoon Andreas Alexios he was living proof of that.

A familiar ache pushed against his ribs. Sometimes it felt like a hollowed-out space inside his chest—an agonisingly silent, still vacuum that nothing could ever quite fill. Other times it throbbed like a bruise. But it was always there, and he'd learned to live with that sense of being incomplete, of being on the outside looking in, surplus to requirements.

Only now he had a chance to change that.

Despite his matrimonial lapse, Andreas was a traditional Greek man. A patriarch from one of Greece's oldest shipping families. He was also ill and, faced with his own mortality, was looking at his legacy.

A legacy that didn't include a legitimate male heir with his bloodline.

Which was why he was now ready to welcome his illegitimate son into the Alexios clan.

After thirty-two years, four months and ten days, Andreas had decided he wanted his only son in whatever was left of his life.

The thought rang a single jarring note in his head. As a child he had always known that Richard Kane wasn't his father, and he had fantasised endlessly about meeting the man who was. Of course, when it had happened, nothing had gone as he'd imagined. It had been like meeting a stranger. A cool-eyed, patrician stranger.

Only now that same stranger was promising him legitimacy and acceptance.

On one condition.

He wanted his only son to settle down and marry. And, although it had been more hinted at than formally discussed, to produce the heirs that would ensure the patrilineal continuation of the house of Alexios.

Achileas felt his breathing stall. If only it was that easy.

He thought back to Tamara's histrionics.

Maybe it could be. She was wealthy, beautiful, and good in bed. Plus, she wanted things to get more serious. Well, it didn't get more serious than marriage. If he asked her to be his wife, he knew she would say yes in a heartbeat.

But the truth was he didn't want to marry Tamara. As for having children... That wasn't an option. How could a man who had never known his own father possibly know how to be a father himself?

Either way, he was sick and tired of relationships in general, and more specifically relationships with women who thought they could get their own way by yelling and crying and stamping their feet.

His eyes dropped to the woman looking up at him now. Not that this one was yelling or crying.

But apparently Effie Price was expecting him to apologise.

Aware of his bodyguards' carefully averted gazes, he felt a pulse of anger beat across his skin as he stared down at her.

Just who did she think she was talking to? More importantly, who was she to talk to him in this way?

I mean, look at her, he thought dismissively, his gaze skimming her flat shoes and cheap bag. *And as for that dress... It looks like something favoured by early nineteenth-century missionaries.*

If she hadn't walked into him, he would have walked straight past her. His eyes drifted over her small oval face. And yet she seemed familiar for some reason...

The frustration of the last few hours reverberated inside him and he felt something snap. He was tired and hungry and in a hurry. The last thing he needed right now was to be lectured by Little Miss Nobody.

'That's not going to happen,' he said softly.

She blinked owlishly behind the thick lenses of her glasses and there was a moment of silence. Then she lifted her chin, and he felt a sudden, wholly unexpected stirring of lust as his gaze slid down the soft curve of her throat.

'Then you and I have nothing more to say to one another,' she said primly. 'So, if you could just give me back my bag, I have somewhere to be.'

Achileas gritted his teeth. *She* was dismissing *him*.

He stared down at her, too stunned to speak,

his pulse juddering like a needle across a record. *Nothing more to say?* No, that wasn't how this worked. He always had the last word.

'*Excuse me, sir?*'

It was Crawford, the head of his security detail.

'What is it?' he snarled, without turning.

'We have a situation, Mr Kane. Apparently, Ms Ivanov has called her brother and he's heading this way.'

Achileas swore under his breath.

Of course he was.

And, knowing Roman as he did, no doubt he would make a monumental scene.

His mouth thinned. No way: not now and not here.

Normally it wouldn't bother him in the slightest. He thrived on conflict and confrontation. It was one of the reasons he'd gone from business school graduate to hedge fund billionaire before the age of thirty.

But Andreas Alexios was pathologically averse to scandal. That was, after all, why he, his bastard son, had grown up with another man's name.

He felt the ache in his chest spread like an oil spill. It had all been sorted out long before he was born. Pretty much about the time his mother had found out she was pregnant a team of lawyers had arrived with an NDA, and in return for her silence she had received a generous financial settlement.

Of course, he knew now that that amount could have been multiplied tenfold and still not made a dent in the Alexios fortune. But what stung more than that was the fact that his father had sat down with his lawyers and carefully and precisely calculated the cost of abandoning his child. Just enough to ensure his son would always be comfortably provided for, to make him socially acceptable. But not enough so that he could stand on an equal footing with his half-sisters and cousins.

Or course that had changed. He had changed it through hard work and determination. And pushing his ambition, obsessively driving that hunger to succeed, to win, had been an unspoken need to best Andreas so that he no longer needed his father's wealth.

Nor did he want a relationship with Andreas. The years when he had wanted and needed a father were long gone.

What he wanted was revenge. Retribution for being ignored for so long. A reckoning, in fact. Taking what was his by right. Taking back what he was owed. Besides, the Alexios name would be good for business. *His* business. And that was all that mattered to him.

Losing his temper with Roman was a luxury he would have to forgo right now. He couldn't risk giving his father a reason to back off, and if that meant walking away from a fight, then so be it.

But it was galling not to have the last word.

He frowned at the thought, and then Effie Price looked up at him and he saw himself reflected in her glasses. Saw himself as she was seeing him. A narrow-eyed, unshaven surly stranger, looming over her.

Except that he wasn't in the wrong here.

'As it happens, I have plenty to say,' he said, focusing his temper and frustration on the woman in front of him.

There was a beat of silence and then her mouth pulled into a frown. 'Then perhaps it's your hearing that needs testing, Mr Kane,' she said, giving him another glimpse of her throat as her face tilted up to meet his. 'Because I just told you I have somewhere to be.'

The flush to her cheeks made her look almost pretty, and he gazed down at her, momentarily startled by both that thought and by the ripple of heat that skimmed across his skin in response to it.

'There's nothing wrong with my sight or my hearing, Ms Price. In fact, there's nothing wrong with any part of me.'

'Apart from your ego.' One delicate eyebrow arched upwards. 'That seems a little swollen…

bloated, even. You might want to go and see a doctor about it.'

In comparison to the insults and accusations Tamara had flung at him earlier, it was nothing. So why did it sting so much? Why did he feel the need not just to deny her accusation but to prove her wrong?

Not knowing or wanting to know the answer to either question, he glanced away to where his bodyguards stood, waiting at a respectful distance.

This was ridiculous.

Roman could show up at any moment, and if that happened the fallout could easily derail his potential rapprochement with his father. And yet, for some reason he couldn't explain, he was still reluctant to end the conversation.

From inside the hotel, he heard the thunder of footsteps, and his shoulders tensed as he saw his bodyguards' heads snap as one towards the doors.

'Sir—'

Crawford stepped forward again. His head of security was a professional. Ex-Special Forces. His face was smooth and unreadable, but there was no mistaking the note of urgency in his voice now.

'We need to move.'

He glanced down at Effie Price.

In the dappled London light, she looked soft

and small and young. Imagining Roman's explo-
sive temper ricocheting around her in this quiet
side street, Achileas felt a stab of irritation. He
couldn't leave her to face that alone. But if he
didn't leave now, who knew what she would see
and hear? And the last thing he needed was a
witness.

So, take her with you...

Later he would wonder what had possessed
him to follow through on that entirely random
thought, but in the heat of the moment it seemed
not only rational but imperative that she go with
him.

'You heard the man.' He turned towards her.
'We need to move.'

Her eyes flew to his, but she didn't move. In
fact, to his immense irritation, she seemed to dig
her small feet into the pavement.

'Move...?' Staring up at him, Effie Price repeated the word slowly, almost as if she needed
to say it out loud to confirm what she'd heard.
'What are you talking about?'

Behind him, raised male voices filtered into
the street, indistinct but unmistakably Russian,
and the footsteps were closer now—purposeful,
unwavering.

It was crunch time.

He took a step forward. 'It's really quite simple. I need to leave. And you're coming with me,'
he said firmly.

Her eyes widened cartoonishly and she opened her mouth to protest, but it was too late. He had already tossed her bag onto the back seat and, ignoring her soft gasp of surprise, he ushered her into the car and slid smoothly in beside her.

CHAPTER TWO

EFFIE FELT HER HEART leap into her throat as the car door slammed shut. Seconds later the huge black SUV began to move.

She couldn't believe what was happening.

One moment she'd been standing on the pavement...the next Achileas Kane had been propelling her into the car and she had obeyed, driven not by the hand guiding her but by the sheer force of his personality.

And now she was lying across the back seat of his car, his body wedged alongside hers, muscular legs a hair's breadth away from her thighs, his right arm resting lightly across her waist.

Just as if they were in bed together.

Thinking about her neatly made bed with its faded quilt, she felt her cheeks burn hot against the cool leather seat. As if a man like him would share *her* bed. Only Jasper had ever done that. And he was a cat.

Her breath caught.

This couldn't be real. Things like this happened to other people—not her. Her life had always been so small and contained. But none of that changed the fact that this was happening. To her. *Now.*

She swallowed against the mix of emotions rising in her throat and finally, when she got her breathing under control again, she said quietly, 'What exactly do you think you're doing?'

'I believe it's called an extraction.'

His voice was close, and deep, and she felt it move through her. Maybe if it had just been the nearness of his body she could have stayed remote—after all, she couldn't actually see him. But this close she couldn't block out the scent of him, and she had been right. There was lavender and caramel. But there was also the scent of his skin—clean, warm…

Closing her eyes, she breathed in shakily.

Male.

'Keep your head down.'

Her eyes snapped open. No *please*, she noted. Then again, it wasn't a request but an order, given by a man who had never had to ask for anything. Probably he'd never thanked anyone either. Why would he? No doubt he had been raised from birth believing he was entitled to the life he led. Who would he feel the need to thank?

She couldn't see much through the tinted glass window, but she heard the hotel doors burst open

and then a man's voice, bellowing like a maddened bull.

'Where the hell is he?' he roared. *'Achileas!
Achileas!'*

There was a quivering silence like the hush
before the start of a play, and then he bellowed
again—a furious, tumbling tirade of words in a
foreign language... Russian maybe. It sounded
like either a curse or a challenge. Amplified by
his anger and frustration, the man's howls reverberated down the street, and even though the
car was moving, Effie couldn't stop herself from
shivering.

'You don't need to be frightened. Trust me,
his bark is worse than his bite.'

Achileas's deep voice cut through the pounding of her heartbeat, and she felt the scratch of
his stubble against the shoulder of her dress as
he adjusted his position.

'I'm not frightened,' she said quietly, and she
was surprised to find that she was telling the
truth.

Only that didn't make much sense, because
surely, she should be frightened. After all, she
had just been bundled into a car by a complete
stranger. But—and this made no sense at all—
he was the reason she wasn't scared.

Stunned, surprised, but not scared.

She cleared her throat and edged away from
him—away from the hypnotic, destabilising pull

of his scent. 'But nor am I particularly inclined to trust anything you say, Mr Kane. Given that you just dragged me off the street in broad daylight.'

'A necessary precaution,' he said, batting away her accusation with the expert dexterity of a lion flicking away flies with his tail. 'My head of security had information that a situation was developing. I didn't want you to get caught in the crossfire.'

His arm shifted against her and every nerve in her body went haywire, her skin pulling so tightly around her bones it felt like she had been shrink wrapped.

'I thought you said his bark was worse than his bite?'

She felt him hesitate. His irritation buffeted the car's interior. 'I did say that, and I was telling the truth. Roman Ivanov isn't violent, but he is volatile, and right now he's a little upset.'

As if to prove the point, another barrage of invective rippled down the street.

'With you, apparently.'

The muscles in his forearm bunched beneath his jacket. 'Yes, Miss Marple, with me. But it's not a big deal.'

'It sounds like it's a big deal to him.'

Abruptly he shifted away from her. She sat up, smoothing her hair away from her face. He watched her in silence, his blue gaze cool and assessing. His mouth—that beautiful, sensual curve—flattened into a line, and then he shrugged.

'He makes a lot of noise, but I've dealt with far worse. It comes with the territory.' His lips curved again, but he wasn't smiling. 'Home invasion. Kidnapping. Carjacking. I've had people threaten to burn down my house. *While I'm in it*. Not that I'd expect you to know what that feels like.'

Which, roughly translated, meant that he was rich and important; and she was not.

She stared at him for a long moment. 'I don't have to know,' she said quietly. 'I don't make a habit of upsetting people.'

He leaned back against the leather upholstery and stared at her steadily, a muscle pulsing in his cheek. 'It was nothing,' he said finally. 'Just a misunderstanding.'

There was a gritty silence. Effie thought back to the beautiful blonde-haired woman in the lift.

She might be inexperienced when it came to men but being a virgin didn't mean she was stupid. And you couldn't work as a chambermaid in a hotel like the Stanmore and not have your eyes opened. Or recognise a mess when you saw one.

Achileas's mess just happened to be a tall, leggy blonde instead of a pile of discarded towels.

At a guess, the woman was most likely the angry Russian's girlfriend. Or wife. Hence his bellowing fury. Not that it was any of her business.

She lifted her chin. 'Did he not look where he was going either?'

For a moment he didn't reply, and she held her breath as the silence in the car swallowed up her words. He did this, she thought. He was like a black hole, so intense and powerful that everything around him just buckled to his will.

'When you said you weren't frightened, I didn't believe you...'

His voice was soft with a huskiness that made her shiver.

'But you're not, are you?'

As his eyes arrowed into hers Effie felt her toes curl up in her shoes. Their intensity made her skin sting. Nobody had ever looked at her like that before—properly, intently, as if he was peeling off not just her uniform but her skin. As if he was *seeing* her.

Her heart thudded beneath her uniform. Her stomach was trembling with panic—far more panic than she'd felt when he jostled her into the car. Not because of his question, but because for the first time in her entire life she wasn't just a daughter or a maid or even a wannabe entrepreneur.

She was a woman.

An unfamiliar heat tiptoed across her skin, and she stared up at him, giddy with the utter newness of the sensations she was feeling. She had lied to him. He did scare her a little. But only like a deer caught in the dazzling beam of headlights. He was just too perfect. Too real. Too solid. Too close.

Too much.

Mostly, though, she was scared of herself.

This morning she had woken up and got dressed and come to work and she had known exactly who she was. Now she was struggling to remember. It was as if she was losing shape, growing soft, melting...

Moments earlier she had thought it was panic. But she knew panic, and it wasn't that pounding through her like a dizzying roll of thunder. This was something else. Something she had never felt or expected to feel. A kind of life-changing fire in her blood that consumed everything in its flames.

Her heart froze mid-beat.

Including the most important meeting of her life.

She gazed past him blindly, a flood tide of shock and dismay sweeping through her. The appointment at the bank had been centre stage and at the front of her mind for so long, and yet in just a few unsettling minutes this man—this stranger—had erased it.

And she had helped him. Like a child seeing something shiny and out of reach, in thrall to the wildfire of yearning he had provoked, she'd let herself be distracted, jeopardising her hopes, her plans, her future.

Abruptly she shook her head. 'Why would I be frightened, Mr Kane? You don't strike me as dangerous or depraved.' She took a breath. 'Just arrogant and thoughtless.'

He was staring down at her, eyes narrowed, his forehead creasing as if he couldn't believe what she was saying. Which was understandable, as she couldn't quite believe it either.

There was a tense, electric pause and then he said softly, 'I didn't ask your opinion of me, Ms Price.'

'And I didn't ask for this, Mr Kane.' She gestured around the SUV's luxurious interior. 'You just took me along for the ride.'

He leaned forward now, his blue eyes darkening like the sea before a storm. 'Along for the ride?' he repeated slowly. 'You heard Ivanov. I was doing you a favour,' he said, with all the sensitivity and self-awareness of a man unaccustomed to being either. 'What would you rather? That I'd left you there?'

She swallowed, her throat suddenly scratchy. *No.* And not because she had felt the warmth of his muscle-hard body next to hers or breathed in the to-die-for scent of his skin.

Her stomach flipped over and she remembered her appointment with the bank manager. She thought about all the beds she'd stripped.

The bins she had emptied and the toilets she'd scrubbed. Then she pictured the empty chair where she should be sitting. She clenched her teeth.

'Yes, I would have preferred that. I was supposed to be meeting someone at the bank. It was important.'

His face hardened. It was like watching molten bronze cool.

'*You* have an important meeting?'

She felt her cheeks flush.

'*Had* an important meeting.' She pressed her hand against the door to steady herself. It wasn't strictly true, but it would be by the time she got back to the hotel and retrieved her phone. 'Thanks to you, I've missed it.'

He made a gesture of impatience. 'If it was so important, why didn't you mention it before?'

'I did mention it,' she protested, the unfairness of his remark making her breath judder against her ribs. 'I told you I had to be somewhere, but you didn't listen to me.'

His face was hard. 'You're a grown woman, Ms Price. If you want to be listened to then maybe you should make more of an effort to be heard.'

'In that case,' she said, squaring her shoulders, 'I'd like you to take me back to the hotel. No—on second thoughts, you can just drop me here. That way you won't have to worry about running into Mr Ivanov.'

He straightened then, and as his gaze narrowed on her face she saw the flame in his eyes, the smouldering male pride.

'As you wish,' he said, staring down at her, suddenly ferociously cold and hard and hostile.

She felt the hair on her nape rise as he snapped out something in Greek, and within seconds the huge car slid to a stop.

As the bodyguard in the passenger seat got out to open her door, she picked up her bag.

'Take care, Ms Price.'

His deep voice pulled her back into the cool interior, and she turned, her eyes locking with his.

'I'm not the one hiding, Mr Kane,' she said quietly.

His face changed. He looked startled—*no*, actually, what he looked was winded, as if instead of speaking she had landed a punch to his gut.

But then the door opened, and she was on the pavement, walking and then running, pushing through the lunchtime shoppers, moving as fast and as far as she could from his furious sapphire gaze.

I'm not the one hiding.

Jaw clenching, Achileas lifted the glass of whisky—his second—and threw back the contents, a pulse of anger beating erratically across his skin. Tension was part of his life. His work both generated and required it. But he had never been this tense—ever.

After Effie had got out of the car, he had been so incensed that he hadn't been able to speak. When finally, his voice had returned, he had curtly told his driver to take him to his apartment—one of the four homes he owned at strategic points around the globe.

His lip curled. Properties, not homes.

He didn't have a home. Not now, not ever.

His stepfather, Richard Kane, had been in the US military, and as a consequence the family had moved around a lot. Until the marriage had ended. And then shortly afterwards he'd been sent to boarding school in England.

The tension in his shoulders spread down his spine, knotting at the base of his back, new pain mingling with the old.

Boarding school had finished what his stepfather had started, effectively turning him into a nomad, a citizen of nowhere. A small boy with a suitcase that for a long time had been bigger than he was.

Returning to the States at the end of the first term, he'd found that as well as another new home he had a new stepfather—Mike. But by the time he'd left school, Mike was long gone. His mother was never alone for long. *Unlike him.*

Thinking back to the men who had come and gone over the years, he felt the ache in his chest press against his ribs. As it turned out, they had all been pretty interchangeable. After an opening flurry of dad-like activities none of them had bothered pretending they wanted to be a father—not a father to him, anyway.

Then again, why should they? He hadn't belonged to them. Hadn't belonged anywhere. He was like the cat in that Rudyard Kipling story. He walked by himself, and all places were alike to him.

He glanced around the apartment.

Like all his properties, it was real estate gold. Tall ceilings, big windows, plenty of open space, all decorated in largely neutral shades. There were no distinguishing features, no familial photos.

His fingers tightened around the smooth glass tumbler. He would have preferred to go back to the Stanmore, but there was a chance that Roman—or, worse, Tamara—might still be at the hotel and he didn't trust himself to be either calm or kind.

And that incensed him more, for it seemed to validate Effie Price's accusation. Maybe that was why he had been sitting on this sofa for over an hour now. Sitting and stewing over her parting shot.

He gazed morosely out of the penthouse's

panoramic window, his eyes tracking across the skyline, leapfrogging between London's iconic landmarks. There was no reason that he should still be thinking about what Effie had said. She was nothing to him. Aside from her name, he knew nothing about her. And yet he felt as though she was here, sitting beside him, staring at him gravely.

Leaning back against the sofa cushions, his body tense, nostrils flaring, he suddenly knew why he was feeling that way. It was because she *was* here. Or at least her scent was, and it was filling his senses.

He felt his pulse accelerate.

Mostly he wasn't a big fan of women's perfumes, but this one…

Lowering his face, he breathed in the smell of her, heat creeping over his skin. It wasn't overtly seductive or cloyingly floral, like a lot of the perfumes women wore. But then it wasn't really a perfume. Perfume was manmade, stoppered in a bottle in a factory and sold to the masses.

Effie's scent was something more subtle… both delicate and tantalising, like a promise hovering over her skin.

His pulse slowed a little as he remembered the moment when he'd pulled her down onto the seat beside him. Their bodies had barely touched, but her scent had travelled over his skin like the softest caress, so that for a moment he'd had to fight against the urge to pull her close and keep inhaling her scent.

Infuriated by the memory of how near he'd come to losing control, he stood up and stalked across the room and out onto the balcony that wrapped around two sides of his apartment. In the early afternoon sunlight London looked oddly peaceful, with a warm, golden glow gilding the steel-framed skyscrapers and softening the sharp brick edges.

His mouth twisted. If only his father's edict could be similarly softened into something more appealing.

Had this been a business negotiation it would be easy to bat away Andreas's demands. But he couldn't take that chance—couldn't risk his father turning his back on him, couldn't risk losing the chance to get what he was owed.

For weeks now he'd been trying to find a solution. Only, thanks to Effie, instead of focusing on a reconciled future with his father he'd spent the best part of the day brooding over a past he couldn't change.

'Excuse me, Mr Kane.'

Achileas turned. It was Beatrice, his housekeeper.

'What is it?' he snapped.

'I'm sorry to bother you, sir. Crawford found this in the car, and he wondered if you would like him to dispose of it or return it.'

She held out a folder.

He stared at it for a moment, and then took it.

It was cheap-looking, made of plastic. The kind a child might use at school for handing in an essay. Flipping it open, he felt his breath snag on the name at the top of the first page: *Effie Price*.

It was a business proposal for a perfumery. Suddenly he was conscious of the hammering of his heart.

'No,' he said slowly. 'No, leave it with me.'

Walking back into the apartment, he sat on the sofa, put down his glass and started to read, skimming down the page with practised speed.

She was a maid at the Stanmore. That at least explained the dress.

His pulse twitched as he remembered that moment outside the hotel when she had seemed so familiar. He had seen her at work—by the lift. When Tamara had insisted on getting out on the wrong floor. Only she hadn't been wearing glasses then.

Ten minutes later, he shut the folder. It was a pity her missing her meeting because it was an interesting proposition. And she was clearly passionate about perfume and talented to boot, he thought, breathing in the last lingering traces of her scent.

But then again, he would stake his business reputation on her being refused any loan.

Yes, by his standards, the amount she wanted

to borrow was tiny. Unfortunately, however, she had next to no security, and he could see problems with both her cost to revenue ratio and her customer acquisition strategy.

Tipping his head back, he stretched out his neck and shoulders.

None of which mattered to him, of course. He was just procrastinating, avoiding the moment of truth. That after weeks of thinking, deliberating, weighing up the alternatives and generally attempting to resolve the dilemma created by his father's stipulation, he was still no closer to knowing what to do.

And he was running out of time.

Andreas wouldn't—couldn't—wait for ever.

His hand beat out an impatient rhythm against the arm of the sofa. He knew he didn't want to get married, but he needed a wife. And, whoever she was, he needed her to understand that, while legal, their marriage would be just for show. Yet it would have to appear indisputably real to his father.

Only that was the problem.

All of the women he knew would not be willing to just act the part of his wife. They would want it to be real.

The obvious solution was to pay someone. But he could hardly advertise the position on the Arete Equity website. His shoulders slumped. Surely there had to be an answer. Something he'd missed. But after months of fruitless rumination and circular arguments maybe it was time to face facts. Perhaps she didn't exist. This woman who needed money and yet would not be fazed by such an outlandish suggestion.

Or maybe she was right under his nose. He sat forward abruptly and picked up Effie's proposal, a charge of electricity snapping across his skin.

There it was: her address. Praed Gardens. His mind whirred as out of the unsatisfactory and messy randomness of his day so far, an idea slid into diamond-sharp focus inside his head, clean and pure like a drop of rain.

'Beatrice?' He got to his feet as the house-keeper appeared.

'Yes, Mr Kane?'

'Tell Crawford to bring the car round to the front of the building. I have a meeting with someone.'

His fingers flexed against the folder. He could talk to his lawyer en route...

Yanking open her fridge, Effie peered inside. Not that she needed to look. She already knew what was in there. Half a pint of milk, a bag of ready-washed lettuce, some yoghurts that were well past their sell-by date and a jar of tama-rind paste.

Her throat tightened. She had been planning

on ordering a takeaway for tonight—to celebrate. Only now there was nothing to eat. Or celebrate.

She probably should go to the supermarket, but honestly, she couldn't face it right now. She basically wanted today to be over. That was why she was already in her pyjamas. Because the biggest day of her life had turned into the worst.

By the time she got back to the Stanmore, found her phone and called the bank, she was an hour late. All she'd been able to do was apologise. She hadn't told them what had happened— just that she had forgotten the appointment. She could hardly tell them the truth. Who would believe her?

Oh, I forgot my phone, and when I went back to get it one of the guests at the hotel forced me into his car and drove off with me.

She shut the fridge door. Thank goodness she hadn't told her mum that today was the day. Knowing how much it would mean to Sam, she had been badly tempted to do so, but maybe she'd had a sixth sense about how everything would work out. What she should have done was book another appointment, but she was too exhausted.

And she couldn't help thinking that maybe it was fate…that maybe her dreams were just meant to stay dreams.

She swallowed past the lump in her throat. She hadn't cried. She rarely did. In her experience crying rarely changed anything, and there were worse things than missing an appointment with your bank manager.

A lot worse.

She'd seen more than enough of them first-hand. Lived with them and through them.

When she was a child, her father's gambling had always been there in the background. Sometimes he'd stopped for weeks, even months, but then he would come home, his face flushed with triumph, and it would all start up again. The lying, the stealing, the broken promises...

And then her mum had the stroke, her first. Even now she could remember the shock of going to the hospital and seeing the IV drip in her mother's arm.

That day Sam's life had changed for ever. She had never fully recovered. But neither had she given up. She might not be able to tint eyelashes anymore, but she had taught herself to paint— first still-life, then people. Her friends, her carers...

And her daughter.

Glancing over at the portrait her mother had done of her, Effie felt her legs tremble as the misery she had been fighting all afternoon threatened to take her feet out from under her. Despite her frailty, Sam was still her biggest supporter, and getting the loan, getting the business up and running, would have made her mum so happy.

If only she hadn't forgotten her phone. She never had before, but she had been distracted.

Distracted...

Her skin felt suddenly too tight, and as she pictured Achileas's fierce blue gaze a shiver of heat prickled over her.

Would she have forgotten her phone if she hadn't locked eyes with him in the corridor? Probably not. Only then she would never have come back to the hotel. Never bumped into him. Never felt his hand on her waist or breathed in the tantalising scent of his hard, muscular body.

She stared at her portrait. Unlike her, Achileas Kane was unequivocally beautiful, and it was okay to think that. Like admiring a beautiful painting in a gallery. But that didn't take away from how rude and arrogant and full of himself he was.

And yet if she could bottle how he made her feel in those few dizzying moments when he pulled her onto the seat beside him that perfume would be an instant bestseller.

There was a knock at the door.

Oh, no.

She turned and gazed across the room, her heart not just sinking but plummeting like a stone down a well. There was only one person who ever knocked on her door at this time of the day.

Mark worked at the Stanmore too, as a porter. He had an unrequited crush on Emily and wanted to cross-examine Effie about her at every opportunity. To that end, he had taken to dropping in on his way home from work. Normally she just made him a cup of tea and let him talk, but she couldn't face him tonight.

She would just have to pretend she was going out.

Picking up her coat, she pulled it on quickly and unlocked the door.

'Good evening.'

Effie blinked.

It wasn't Mark. It was Achileas Kane, his big body filling the doorframe, his blue eyes fixed intently on her face. For a moment she couldn't breathe, much less speak. How had he managed to find her? More importantly, why was he here?

As if he could read her mind, he held out a folder...*her* folder.

'You left it in my car.' He frowned. 'Are you going out? Or going to bed?'

Her heart fluttering like a moth inside a glass, she stared at him, still lost for words. 'Neither,' she said at last.

His gaze swept assessingly over her in silence. 'In that case, perhaps you could invite me in.'

In where? Into her flat?

She stared at him in shock and confusion, then shook her head. 'I don't let strangers into my flat,

Mr Kane. Just my friends. And people I have to let in. To read the meter or fix the boiler.'

'I see.' He shifted against the frame. 'Well, we might not be friends, but I wouldn't say we were strangers. And if it helps, I could always pretend to read the meter.' There was a beat of silence and then he said quietly, 'Please, Effie.'

It wasn't a big deal. He'd just called her by her name. But something about the way he put the emphasis on the second syllable made her head feel light, and she let the gap between the door and the frame widen.

'Okay, you can come in—but you can't stay long. I have work tomorrow.'

'At the Stanmore.'

'How do you know that? And how did you find out where I live?'

He gave a leisurely shrug as he strolled through the door. 'I read your proposal.'

She stared after him, stunned, almost hating him. 'You had no right. It's private.'

'Which is why I am returning it to you. Did you get to your meeting?'

His intensely blue eyes seemed to pierce her skin, seeing more than she wanted him to—seeing too much. 'No, I didn't.'

'That's a shame. It is a good proposal. A little amateurish, and not nearly ambitious enough, but it is well-argued.'

As he turned slowly on the spot she followed

his gaze, trying to imagine what her small, neat flat must look like to him.

'Did you paint this?'

His eyes had stopped on her portrait, and as he leaned forward her body felt taut and achy... almost as if he was leaning into her.

She shook her head. 'No, my—' She was about to say *my mother*, but he already knew enough about her life from her proposal. She didn't need to reveal anything more to this stunning, arrogant man. 'No, Sam painted it.'

'Sam?' His face stilled. 'Are you in a relationship?'

'No, I'm not.' She shook her head again, turning away to pull off her coat so that he wouldn't see the lie in her eyes. Although it was more just letting him assume something than actually lying. 'Not that it's any of your business.'

'True enough.'

Straightening up, he turned to face her, and she felt goosebumps explode over her skin as his eyes found hers.

'But that could be about to change.'

She stared at him, trying to make sense of his words. 'I'm sorry, Mr Kane—'

'Achileas,' he corrected her. 'I think we've moved past any need for formalities.'

Had they?

Her heart thudded hard, his words accelerating her already racing pulse. 'Maybe...but either way I'm not sure I understand what it is you're trying to say.'

The shifting evening sunlight was licking the miraculous curves of his cheekbones, but his gaze on her face was as dark and powerful and impossible to ignore as a supernova.

'Then let me explain.' He sat down on the sofa and gestured towards the armchair opposite, as if this was his flat, not hers. 'I have a proposition for you. You know the kind of thing—I scratch your back, you scratch mine.'

The small living space seemed to shrink and grow airless as his words swept through her like a forest fire. *Scratch. Back. Yours. Mine.*

'No, I don't think I do know,' she said, trying desperately not to sound as panicked as she felt.

'It's quite simple. I will give you five times what you were asking from the bank. Only it won't be a loan. You won't have to pay a penny of it back.'

Effie blinked. 'You're going to give me five times what I asked for? For nothing?'

'No, not for nothing,' he said, his gaze narrowing in on hers in a way that made her breathing go shallow. 'I need something in return. Something a little, shall we say, unorthodox.'

She stared at him, startled by the word and the flurry of unsettling thoughts it prompted. 'So, what is it that you need?' she said after a moment.

He stretched out his legs and his mouth twisted into a smile that managed to be both mocking and dangerous.

'I need a wife.'

CHAPTER THREE

A WIFE!

Effie stared up at Achileas in stunned silence. She must have misheard him…misunderstood what he was saying. Or was he pranking her?

But as she searched his face, she saw that his expression was no longer mocking but cool and calculating. As if she was some small animal that had blundered into the trap he'd set.

'And you want to marry *me*?'

He frowned, and then, shaking his head, he laughed. Not the nice, warm kind of laughter that accompanied an amusing joke, but the humourless sort that people used when something wasn't funny.

Just wildly implausible to the point of being ludicrous.

Her fingers bit into the folder as she felt it ripple through her.

'Of course I don't want to marry you, Effie. But don't take it personally. I don't want to marry anyone.'

He shifted against the sofa, one muscular arm extending along the cushions. 'I do, however, *need* a wife.'

Now he was making even less sense.

'Need is a strong word, Mr Kane,' she said slowly.

'Achileas,' he corrected her again. 'And maybe you're right. Need *is* too strong a word. Perhaps it would be more accurate to say that I *require* a wife.'

He stretched out his legs, making himself comfortable.

'My father, Andreas, is elderly and very old-fashioned. He has certain expectations, ambitions...' he hesitated '...certain *wishes* for his life, and for his son. And as his son I want to honour those wishes.'

The fog of confusion inside her head suddenly cleared.

'He wants you to get married?'

His dark eyebrows formed a solid line as he nodded. 'Correct. Like I said, he's very old-fashioned. His values are traditional, maybe even a little archaic. But, as someone who's been married for forty years, he believes matrimony is a cornerstone of life.'

Forty years of marriage. That was a good thing, wasn't it? It was a testament to his parents' commitment and love. And yet there was an edge to his voice as if the longevity of their marriage was not a matter of pride or delight, but inconvenience.

She felt suddenly closer to tears than she had all day. Didn't he know how lucky he was? How privileged? To have seen love given and received by two people who had chosen one another. It was as rare and elusive as orris, the precious oil produced from an iris bulb.

She couldn't imagine ever taking that for granted. Being like him. He was so pampered, so entitled…

Except that made him sound like a child—a sulky little boy—and there was nothing boyish about Achileas Kane. He was a man…the physical embodiment of unapologetic masculinity.

'But you don't believe that?' she said.

He shrugged almost lazily, but she could sense a tension that hadn't been there a moment earlier.

'Why would I? Why would anyone? Humans and their ancestors have been walking the planet for about six million years, and for all but a thousand of those years they weren't monogamous. But, as I have explained, matrimony matters to my father. And as he grows older it matters more.'

Her heart thudded as he looked up, his clear blue gaze sharpening against hers. 'And he is getting frailer. That's why I require a wife. Just in the short term,' he added smoothly, as if this somehow made his bizarre request understandable.

Which it didn't.

But why should she care if it was understandable or not? She thought back to his short, derisive bark of laughter, then back further, to when he had told her that she needed to make more effort to be heard if she wanted to be listened to.

Then make him listen, she told herself.

'You might require a wife, Mr Kane, but I don't require a husband. Nor do I want one. Not even in the short term.'

Watching his dark brows snap together, she felt her pulse judder. Was that true? It was certainly true that she had never imagined getting married, but then she hadn't even had a boyfriend yet.

Remembering how she'd let him think Sam had been an ex, she felt her skin burn beneath her pyjamas. The truth was that she only knew a handful of men, and out of those only one husband: her father. And, much as she couldn't stop loving her dad, she would never want to be married to a man like Bill Price. A man who was so addicted to the high of winning that he ended up losing everything. His home. His family. His sanity.

Only that was a whole lot more truth that she was prepared to share with this man now sitting on her sofa. Achileas had bulldozed his way into her life, not once but twice today, and she was still reeling from their last encounter.

Glancing up, she found him looking at her in silence. From where she was standing, he looked relaxed, but she knew that if she got closer, she would see a muscle throbbing in the hard curve of his jaw.

'A wise woman,' he said softly. 'Marriage is for monarchs and fools. It's a plot device in a soap opera. But I'm not offering you a typical marriage, Effie. Our arrangement would be something more pragmatic. Think of it as a mutually beneficial merger of interests.'

A merger of interests.

She stared at him, panic beating in her belly as a cluster of feverishly inappropriate images chased through her head. Damp bodies moving together seamlessly on a tangle of sheets... Bodies peeled naked, hot skin rippling beneath a hand, a tongue—

No.

That wasn't what he meant—and anyway that wasn't who she was. She felt awkward and self-conscious about undressing in front of other women. The idea that she would ever be naked with a man like Achileas made her feel singed inside, and it took every ounce of strength she had not to turn and run to the door.

'We don't share any interests,' she said quickly.

There was a long, uneven silence. Then, 'You think?' He raised one dark eyebrow, considering her.

Claiming her.

She breathed in sharply as every nerve-ending in her body exploded.

That was nonsense. Of course he wasn't claiming her. He wanted to use her to pacify his father and in exchange he was offering her money.

It was a Faustian pact with a blue-eyed devil.

'I thought you wanted to start a business, Effie. I thought it was important to you,' he said now.

The dare in his voice danced over her skin, making her body twitch with fear and fascination.

Her hands clenched. 'It is.'

He stared at her steadily, his blue gaze no longer a sapphire gleam but the glint of tempered steel. 'How important? How badly do you want it? I mean, how far are you prepared to go? Because I can make it happen just like that.'

He snapped his fingers and she blinked.

He could. She glanced down to where he lounged on the sofa. His will was not like hers. It wasn't just an intangible concept. It was a hungry, living thing with a fiercely beating heart.

'Trust me, it will be a lot easier and less painful than dealing with a bank. If you even get that far. Banks are cautious about lending their money. Particularly to new businesses.'

Pulse jumping, she glanced down at his legs, noticing without intending to how the fabric pulled tight around the muscles of his thighs. Thighs that had been inches from hers just a few hours earlier...

'I know that,' she said quietly, hugging the folder protectively against her stomach.

She had read the statistics and they were daunting. Twenty percent of new businesses failed within a year. That went up to a terrifying fifty percent in five years.

'Then you'll also know that they're going to hold your proposal up to the light, and that if they see anything they don't like they will turn you down.'

Effie felt her stomach twist painfully. He was right. Banks weren't charities. And even when she was writing her proposal she had been horribly aware of her lack of experience and security. All she had to offer was an unquantifiable passion and a dream.

What if that wasn't enough?

At least if she agreed to what Achileas was suggesting she would have the money, no questions asked. Questions she might not be able to answer.

But marrying someone you barely knew even in the short term—whatever that meant—wasn't just unorthodox, it was crazy. She would have to be crazy even to consider it.

'Maybe they will,' she said quietly. 'But that's not a reason to marry a man I don't know.'

There was a small, stifling pause.

'So let's get to know each other,' he said softly, and then, more softly still, 'Tell me about yourself, Effie Price. Who are you?'

Staring up at Effie's small, pale face, Achileas felt his breathing jolt.

Why had he asked her that?

It wasn't a question he had ever asked anyone— certainly not a woman. Then again, he had never wanted to know the answer before, and if he did now, it was only for the obvious reason that he needed a wife.

His jaw tightened. *Need*. That word again.

He could play semantics, call it a requirement, but that didn't change the facts. If he wanted the key to his father's kingdom, he needed a wife.

Correction: he needed Effie to be his wife.

Back at his apartment, when the idea had appeared fully formed in his head, he had known there and then that she would be perfect. Why else would fate have thrown them together like that?

Unfortunately, Effie was not coming up with the same answer as he was.

A spasm of tension in his back—the same spasm that had been plaguing him for weeks now—made his shoulders tense against the misshapen fabric-covered lump that was masquerading as her sofa.

He was honest and arrogant enough to admit that he hadn't anticipated her being so resistant to the idea of him as a husband. Obviously, he had known she would be surprised, stunned, speechless… But he was Achileas Kane, founder and CEO of Arete Equity. He was rich, powerful and handsome. And she—well, she just was a chambermaid…a real-life Cinderella to his hedge fund prince. So, after her initial shock had worn off, of course he'd assumed that she would react like any normal woman.

His eyes narrowed on the way Effie was standing, her thin arms clutching the cheap plastic folder in front of her chest like some kind of shield, and he wondered why he had made that assumption.

What was the matter with her? Didn't she know how lucky she was? He was offering to *give* her five times what she was asking from the bank, and instead of being grateful and excited she was staring at him with that same, grave expression on her face as before.

And now she was shaking her head.

'You know who I am.' Her brown eyes hovered on his face. 'You know where I work, how much I earn. You know where I live…how I live,' she said, in that delicate, precise way of hers. 'But if you're serious about this "arrangement", then the question I need answering is, who are *you*?'

For a moment he was stunned, then outraged.

No, that's not how this works, he thought for the second time that day. She didn't get to question him, make him jump through hoops, *judge* him.

Nobody did.

Nobody except one man—the only man he could neither vanquish nor reject because, in spite of everything Andreas had done and not done, it was the saw-toothed ache of his absence that drove Achileas through each day. An ache that was not yet rubbed smooth even though he had turned it over and over endlessly, like an angry sea throwing pebbles against the shore.

He hated how it made him feel so powerless. And now this woman was wanting to know who he was. As if he would ever tell *her*—tell anyone.

It was ludicrous, unthinkable, and he remained stubbornly silent. Having been on the receiving end of his father's silence for so long, he knew first-hand just how effective a weapon it was. But if he didn't answer her, then what?

He glanced over at the tilt of her chin. Incredibly, it seemed that she would refuse his offer and there would be nothing he could do about it.

She might bend, but she wouldn't break.

Like one of those small, thin-stemmed flowers with pale petals that seemed to grow everywhere in England. A wildflower that looked as if one good gust of wind would snap it in two.

But there was strength in those fragile stems. At school, he'd had to endure cross-country runs through the grounds, and after a storm, when everything else had been pulled up by its roots or flattened, those delicate-stemmed flowers had still been upright.

'What do you want to know?' he said slowly.

'I'm not sure...'

She hesitated, and he felt something pinch inside him. Outside the Stanmore, even in the car, she had been so composed, so calm. Now, though, here in her home, with her hair in a plait, and her taut, unblinking gaze, she reminded him of one of those Margaret Keane paintings of huge-eyed waifs. She seemed smaller, younger, wary... And he didn't like how that made him feel.

It was probably just the lighting in her flat.

Or her pyjamas. He had never seen a grown woman wear something so determinedly asexual. His gaze hovered momentarily on where the small, fine bones disappeared beneath her grey top, and he felt his body tighten.

Blanking his mind to what was surely just the consequence of six months of virtual celibacy, he gritted his teeth.

What Effie Price wore in bed was irrelevant to this negotiation.

Effie was an adult, and this was a business deal. And it was a good deal for her. Money aside, she would have access to his world. She would learn how to talk and dress and live like the woman she was pretending to be—and most important of all, after it was all over, she would have her own perfumery business.

He leaned forward slightly, breathing in. Her scent was in no way overpowering. On the contrary, it was elusive. And yet he could feel it tugging at his senses.

'I suppose I'd like to know why me?'

Her voice made his pulse jump and, looking up, he found her brown eyes watching him.

'Why not some other woman? Like the woman you were with at the Stanmore? She's very beautiful.'

'Tamara?' He shook his head, his body tensing automatically at the idea. Tensing in a way that it didn't when he thought of Effie. 'She's beautiful enough, but she's too highly strung.' *Exhaustingly so.* 'That's why I broke up with her. Not today,' he added, although he wasn't quite sure why. 'It was six months ago.'

'But surely there must be other women?'

There were.

A long unbroken stream of glossy-haired socialites like Tamara, or leggy models with bee-stung lips. None had lasted more than three months. Most had lasted a lot less, averaging about a week.

'You have certain qualities they lack,' he said, choosing his words carefully.

Effie was emphatically not his type. Too thin. Too plain. Too quiet. But that was a good thing. He didn't need any distractions. As for sex— This was essentially a business arrangement. He couldn't imagine her offering anything that would make it worthwhile adding *that* extra layer of complication.

'You mean because I'm poor?'

The directness of her words surprised him. But it was true. Her current account balance was pitiful, and her savings amounted to loose change. He glanced around the small living room, seeing the cheapness of everything. And yet that hadn't been his first consideration.

'Partly... But earlier, in the car, you kept your head. I don't know many women—or many men—who would have done that.'

Her clear brown eyes rested on his face. 'And that's what you need. Someone who can keep her head.'

It was a statement, not a question, but he answered it anyway. 'Yes, I do. This has to look real.'

'And what about you?'

She was looking at him, her gaze straight and unblinking.

'What about me?'

'Can you do this? Can you lie to your father and keep your head?'

He felt as if he'd been kicked by a horse.

Lie to his father? Yes, he could easily do that, he thought bitterly. Given that officially Andreas had no son, he was a walking, talking, living lie. His jaw clenched. That was one of the things his father's money had paid for: the Alexios name to be kept off his birth certificate.

But Effie didn't need to know that he was a bastard, and that his future legitimacy was dependent on him marrying. Or that lying to his father was payback for the lie about his birth.

'It won't be a problem,' he said coolly, his blue eyes finding hers. 'All that matters to me is that my father believes I'm happily married.' He tipped back his head. 'So, do we have an agreement?'

The air was suddenly electric, quivering expectantly like a held breath.

Effie looked across to where the man sat, waiting for her to answer. She had chosen that particular sofa because it had been the smallest she could find, the only one that fitted into her flat, and his muscular body made it look like a piece of dolls' house furniture.

Her pulse scampered.

Actually, it wasn't a sofa...it was a loveseat—presumably because couples who were in love were happy to cosy up to one another. But Achileas wasn't in love with her, and she wasn't in love with him—thankfully.

Her heart gave a little shiver of pity for the woman who actually fell in love with Achileas Kane. Not because he was prepared to lie to his father in this way. Sometimes white lies were necessary. They were even forgivable if it meant that they prevented pain or additional suffering. No, what scared her was the ruthlessness and determination that simmered beneath that superbly tailored suit. The relentlessness that was almost elemental. Like a river of molten lava or a hurricane tearing up a city.

He was a man who was used to winning, to getting his own way. A man who didn't understand the concept of no. Her breath trembled in her throat. He made it sound so simple. Marriage for money. And she could see how it might work in theory. But in practice…?

She glanced across the room, her stomach clenching as her gaze settled on the portrait. *Who are you?* Achileas had asked her that question and there was the answer. Small regular features. Straight brown hair. Serious brown eyes. Fresh-faced. Forgettable. Utterly unremarkable.

In other words, not the kind of woman a man like Achileas Kane would ever notice, much less marry.

She bit into her lip. Anybody looking at them

would have that exact same thought. That had been true when he'd cannoned into her outside the Stanmore, and it would stay true. This whole idea was crazy. She didn't even know why they were discussing it.

So why was the conversation still going on? Why had she even let him into her flat? Her insides tightened, blooming with a heat that was unfamiliar and seductive. Discomforting.

'Effie?'

Her name on his lips pulled her in and she turned to face him, the heat spreading to her cheeks.

He was why.

He affected her. He was like the most delicious, irresistible scent teasing her senses, and just for a moment she closed her eyes and breathed him in, let herself be swept away to a Mediterranean island—

But it was time to put the stopper back in the bottle.

Achileas Kane might be a man who didn't understand the meaning of no, but he was going to have to learn. Because he was wrong about her. She couldn't do this even if he could.

She took a breath to steady her nerves. 'Thank you for bringing back my folder, but I think I'll take my chances with the bank.'

He stared at her, his gaze rolling over her like an ocean wave. 'I think that would be a mistake.'

She shook her head. 'No, what would be a mistake would be trying to make this work.'

'It will work,' he said stubbornly, as she had known he would.

And then he pushed up from the sofa and rose, the simple movement carrying with it such an extraordinary impression of power that she took a step backwards. As he stopped in front of her, she felt breathless and off-balance. She had never been confronted by anyone with such a sense of purpose.

'It will work because my father will see what he wants to see.'

'And what if he guesses the truth?' she asked quietly.

'He won't,' he said, looking down at her, his fierce certainty buffeting her so that she had to dig her heels into the carpet to stop herself from stumbling backwards. 'How could he?'

'Easily,' she said quietly, heat breaking out on her skin as his eyes locked onto hers.

Did she need to spell it out?

'You can't really think that anyone will believe we're a couple? Especially your father—the man who raised you.' She cleared her throat. 'I'm not exactly your type, am I?'

There was a short, jangling pause, and then his gaze darkened and narrowed in on hers. 'Not historically, no. But I wasn't looking for a wife before.'

He wasn't looking for one now. Not a real one. Only at some point, if she agreed to this, she would have to act like a wife. They would have to look as if they were in love. Not in private, but in public, they would have to look and talk and touch like lovers.

But how could she do that when she had never been in love? Never been intimate with a man.

Her breath frayed in her throat. 'We can't just tell people we love each other. We'll have to show them. And—'

His gaze narrowed fractionally. 'And what?' he prompted.

She swallowed, shifted. 'I'm not sure I can do that.'

Actually, she was certain she couldn't. Her only experience of kissing a man had been brief and botched and bumbling.

He stared at her for a long moment, then took a step closer—close enough that even in the fading light she could see the stubble forming on his jaw, the flecks of green and gold in his eyes.

'In that case we have a problem. For this to work we both need to feel sure…'

There was a shimmering beat of silence.

'But maybe I could help,' he said softly.

Something was happening. The room was changing, shrinking, growing darker. She was changing too. Her body was humming. She could feel tremors of heat pulsing through her, swirling up inside her like flames drawn up a chimney.

What did he mean? How could he help—?

Her brain stalled, her heart stopped as his lips brushed against hers. And then his hand slid over her jaw to cup her cheek, and he lowered his head and fitted his mouth to hers.

It was like a thousand stars exploding. She felt all breath leave her body. Around her the air grew thick and heavy. Inside, everything started to melt.

Her eyelashes fluttered shut. This was nothing like any kiss she had experienced or could have imagined. His mouth was hot and hard, and the touch of his lips sent a fierce tingling heat straight to her belly. She arched helplessly against him, her hips meeting his, her fingers scrabbling against his arm, blindly, greedily kissing him back.

He made a rough sound in his throat, wrapping his hand around her waist and pulling her closer. The hard press of his body made flames roar through her, burning everything in their path, her hopes, the failure of her day, all logical thought so that there was nothing except Achileas and this devastating, demanding fire of need and longing…

'Effie—'

He pulled her closer, then moved back, pushing her away as if in some strange, one-sided tug-of-war. Opening her eyes, she looked up at him dazedly. His hand was still cupping her face, but the blue of his eyes was rolling back like a tide turning.

Stunned, made mute by what had just happened and by its abrupt ending, she glanced past him, trying to steady herself, to get her bearings. In the early evening sunlight, her flat looked both familiar and yet strange and new, almost as if she was in a dream.

But her grip on his arm was real. And so was that kiss.

A few tendrils of her hair had escaped to curl loosely against her collarbone, and she watched, mesmerised, as he reached out and wound one round his finger.

'Problem solved,' he said softly. 'All we have to do is agree to the terms of our arrangement and then we sign a contract, you sign an NDA, and we're good to go.'

She stared up at him, fighting to keep her tremulous, lambent reaction to him to herself. Because of course it hadn't been real for him. He had simply wanted to prove a point—and he had.

Unequivocally.

'So, do we have an agreement?'

His voice was rough, impatient, and she felt her stomach clench. But it would be different next time. *She* would be different. She would know what to expect. Besides, when they were alone and behind closed doors there would be no need to kiss at all, and they wouldn't kiss like that in public.

They weren't going to kiss like that ever again.

This deal was not about kissing. It was about easing an old man's mind, and it was about money, and afterwards she would have money. Real money. Enough to set up her business and give her mum the kind of care and comfort she deserved.

And okay, it was 'unorthodox', perhaps even a little crazy but it wouldn't be like her parents' marriage, and that was what she dreaded the most. Ending up in a relationship where nothing was as it seemed. Where trust and truth were vague, treacherous, shifting sands. At least this marriage to Achileas would have clear boundaries. Strict rules of engagement. There would be no secrets or lies between them.

Inside her head she heard a tiny click, like the hands of a clock stopping, and she let her gaze wander round the room, seeing it as if she had never looked at it before. This morning she had woken up thinking today would be the first day of her new life. It was what she'd hoped and planned for so long.

And now there was this. There was *him*. Achileas.

He hadn't been part of that plan...

But he could be.

'Yes. We have an agreement,' she said quietly, and she felt a sharp rush of adrenaline and an eager anticipation that startled her with its intensity.

A flicker of triumph darkened his eyes to black. 'I'll have the paperwork sent over.'

CHAPTER FOUR

THIS WAS EXACTLY what he needed, Achileas thought, stepping onto the balcony that led off his bedroom and into the warm, fluttering air. After the fast-food and exhaust-fume-filled grey air of London there was something cleansing about the bright beat of the sun.

Greek sunlight was laser-white and hot—so hot that even wearing loose linen trousers and a T-shirt he felt overdressed.

He squinted through the light to where the sapphire sparkle of the sea met the cloudless blue sky, letting his eyes adjust, and then he caught a movement down on the sleek stone terrace. He tensed as a small, slight figure in a pale ankle-skimming dress and a cartwheel-sized straw hat stepped into view.

Effie.

He felt his breath catch.

It was just over a week since he had knocked on the door to her Lilliputian flat and asked her to be his wife. It had taken eight days to extricate her from her job, and get the legal documents written up and signed before flying first to Athens on his private jet and then by helicopter to the island.

His island.

He stared out across the terrace, his gaze leap-frogging over the low stone wall that edged the pool area to the untouched landscape of wind-tangled cedar and feathery grasses, and further still to the smooth, wide strip of never-ending blue.

It was nearly seven years since he'd bought this tiny outcrop of rock at the edge of the Cyclades, and he still wasn't tired of the view. Truthfully, it was the only place on the planet where he stopped to notice the view. Perhaps that was why he came closest here to feeling at home.

It wasn't just the view. There was a serenity and a simplicity that both soothed and invigorated him. And, of course, privacy. His mouth twisted. Maybe it was a hangover from shared dormitories at school, but he liked to have his own space.

Except now it wasn't just his space.

Out on the terrace, Effie was making her way around the edge of the gleaming turquoise infinity pool. He watched her, his eyes narrowing on the sway of her hips as she moved. But his body was remembering the feel of those hips when he'd kissed her and she had kissed him back, arching against him, her body curving like a bow in his hands.

His fingers tightened against the rail. He had kissed her to prove her wrong. Instead, *he* had been proved wrong.

Tracking her progress across the smooth slabs, he felt his pulse speed up. She had tasted sweet like honey, and she had been so responsive. That was what had shocked him most—what shocked him now. He had thought she would be prim and proper, and there had been a kind of hesitancy at first, but then she had melted into him, against him.

He could feel it now. *Still.*

And he hadn't been able to hold back. Hadn't wanted to stop. It had taken a massive effort of will to pull away from her body, to tear his mouth from hers, and even then, he had struggled to hide the truth of things.

He jammed his hands in his pockets. It was his own fault. The self-inflicted consequence of six months of celibacy. And it wouldn't happen again. She wasn't his type.

But she was going to be his wife.

Only for that to work they needed to get comfortable with one another. Comfortable enough for him to be able to confidently introduce Effie to his father. The corners of his mouth curved into a small, satisfied smile.

Then, finally, he would be rightfully, publicly

and legally acknowledged for what and who he already was. *An Alexios.*

It couldn't happen soon enough, he thought with a flicker of impatience. Now that he had a wife waiting in the wings, he just wanted it done. So, there would be no diving into the pool and swimming a few leisurely lengths as he would normally. He had told Effie to meet him for breakfast. He wanted to go over the story of how they'd first met.

His gaze dropped to the woman who would be joining him—only Effie wasn't there. His smile stiffened as he caught sight of her hat, disappearing out of view. Apparently, she had somewhere else to be. Somewhere he wasn't.

Blue.

Blue everywhere as far as the eye could see.

Effie turned slowly on the spot, blinking in the sunlight. Without her glasses it was almost like being underwater.

She had never experienced such an intensity or variety of one colour. It was as if after waking this morning she'd found her world had switched from monochrome to colour. The sky was a sweep of harebell-blue, darkening to navy where it merged with the sea. And the sea—

Holding her breath, she took a hesitant step towards the edge of the path and gazed down over the edge of the rockface. Up until this moment, the only sea she had ever seen in person had been on a rare holiday to Great Yarmouth. The North Sea had been wet and salty and vast, but that was where any resemblance to the expanse of water in front of her ended.

She stared in silence at the miracle of the Aegean, almost unbelieving. There was so much light, and even though the sea didn't seem to be moving every time she looked it was different, each rippling wave catching the sun's rays and making it shimmer like a gemstone so that there wasn't just blue but silver and gold.

And then there was the air.

Back in England, she'd never thought about breathing, and she knew that the air she was breathing here must be the same mix of oxygen and nitrogen. Only how could that be? Had it been washed in the sea? Was that why it was as soft and clean as freshly laundered sheets? There was salt and thyme and rosemary… It was as if the island itself was breathing—

Her head was spinning. It was too much.

But then should she be surprised, given who owned the island?

A shiver, not of cold but of heat, that had nothing to do with the quivering white sun, ran down her spine. *Too much.* That was what she had thought about Achileas in the car when he had looked over at her and everything had stopped. Then dissolved.

Her bones, her breath.

Her sense of self-preservation.

But locking eyes with him had been a warm-up act. His kiss had knocked the world off its axis and sent it spinning into space and she was still scrabbling to get back on her feet. And now she was here with him on this island—*his private island*—surrounded in every direction by a sea as mesmerizingly blue as his gaze.

She stared fixedly at the horizon, using it as a spirit level to steady herself.

Over the last few days, she had refused to let herself think about that moment in the flat, concentrating instead on practicalities. Like packing and getting a passport.

She hadn't told anyone what she was doing. Not the official version and certainly not the truth.

At work, it had been easy to let Emily and Janine and Mark believe that she was leaving to start her business. Which was sort of true. But when it had come to her mum, she had said nothing about that. As far as Sam was concerned, she was taking a well-deserved holiday.

Her hands curled at her sides. She didn't tell lies, and lying to people she cared about—to her mum in particular—was horrible. More horrible still was knowing that she could do it with such ease. Remembering how effortlessly the lies had spilled from her father's mouth, she felt her stomach knot. She didn't want to be a chip off that particular block.

But in spite of the lies, and the quivering, slippery panic she felt whenever she thought about being alone with Achileas, it would be worth it in the end. Picturing the rows of bottles in her yet to be opened flagship store, she felt a sudden, unfiltered upswing of happiness. It was going to be all right.

First, though, she had to get to know her husband-to-be.

In fact, she was supposed to be doing that now, she thought, a prickling panic darting over her skin as she realised the time.

Turning, she began to walk back along the path, quickly at first, and then more hesitantly. Distracted by the light and the sea and the air, she hadn't been paying much attention to where she was, and now she wondered if she had gone the wrong way.

She was on the verge of retracing her steps when a breeze from the sea whipped at her hat. Reaching up, she snatched at it, laughing, feeling a rush of exhilaration rising inside her at the absurdity and newness of it all.

And then suddenly, just as her fingers curled around the rim, he was there.

Blue-eyed, dark-jawed, even darker scowl.
Achileas.

They almost collided again. Just in time she took a hurried step sideways and—

She gasped, her eyes widening, her exhilaration switching to fear as the ground seemed to be cut away beneath her and she felt herself starting to fall.

And she would have kept on falling if Achileas hadn't caught her arm, clamping his hand painfully around her elbow to jerk her to safety.

Although safety was relative where he was concerned, she thought a moment later, her pulse twitching out of time.

Looming over her, his face was starkly furious in the daylight. And he was swearing more than she had ever heard anyone swear in her life. Not that she understood what he was saying as she didn't speak Greek, but she didn't need to.

Only it wasn't his anger that was making her pulse stumble. It was the jewelled brilliance of his eyes and the hard heat of his very male body. It felt so intimate, even though there had been no intimacy between them.

Except for that kiss, she thought, remembering his hard, insistent mouth and the surge of devastating, irrational hunger that had swept through her body to pool deep in her core. She felt goosebumps rise along her arms as his gaze locked on hers, eyes narrowing as if he too was reliving those frantic, feverish moments—

Abruptly, he let go of her arm.

'Do you ever look where you're going?' he demanded, swapping to English with a fluency that, despite her panicky heartbeat, she found herself envying.

'Do you?' she countered.

His eyebrows snapped together. 'I was looking where I was going. More importantly, I was also on time for our meeting this morning. Unlike you.'

He stared down at her, a muscle pulsing in his cheek. Beside them, the sea kept on being the sea, and she wondered if he was regretting bringing her. Or just contemplating throwing her in.

'I need you to pay attention, Effie, because I'm only going to say this once,' he said at last, his voice gratingly harsh in the whispering breeze. 'This is not some holiday. We made a deal. I am investing in your business and in return you will be my wife. But for that to be believable we need to spend some time together. So, when I say I'll see you at breakfast, I'm not asking you.' His blue gaze locked onto hers. 'I'm paying you. Is that clear?'

To be fair, it had been clear before. Only, stupidly, she had thought that there was an equality of sorts in their arrangement. But to him she was only a cog in the wheel of a machine, brought here to serve a purpose.

His purpose.

Because, of course, Achileas was the machine.

She gazed up at him, her heart beating in her throat. Sunlight was caressing his cheekbones and the line of his jaw reverently, like an adoring lover. But no amount of sun could disguise the hard, uncompromising set of his features.

'Perfectly.'

Her response was automatic, her voice as quiet and placating as it would have been if she was at work and he was a dissatisfied guest, but she felt a flicker of defiance as she spoke. As a maid she was truly just a cog, a tiny moving part. But wasn't a wife—even a fake one—by definition a partner?

'Good.' His brooding gaze held hers momentarily. 'Then let's get back to the villa. We've wasted enough time this morning already.'

It was on the tip of her tongue to point out that they could use the time it would take to walk back to the villa to get to know one another, but he had already turned and stalked off down the path. And, as it turned out, it took considerably less time to get back than it had taken her to reach the sea.

Achileas walked swiftly and with the same intensity of purpose with which he seemed to do everything else, eating the ground with his long, fluid strides, only pausing occasionally and impatiently for her to catch up.

It was as if he was in a race. But where was the finishing line? More importantly, what was the prize? Surely there were only so many houses and private jets and islands you could buy, she thought.

Back at the villa, breakfast was waiting for them on the beautiful stone terrace.

Effie sat down at the table and, like a member of an orchestra tuning up for a performance, her stomach started to rumble.

It was nothing like the breakfast she ate at home, she thought, gazing down at the array of plain white bowls and platters, filled with soft, billowing peaks of yogurt, freshly sliced fruit and delicious pastries dusted with icing sugar.

But, despite her hunger, it was the house that drew her gaze.

She had seen it last night, when they'd arrived on the island, but she had been too tired—not just from the journey but from the days leading up to it—to register much about the exterior except that it wasn't quite what she had imagined.

To her, Greek architecture was either a ruined temple with lots of columns or those postcard-pretty white houses with blue doors and domed roofs. But the Villa Elytis was neither a ruin nor white. It was a soft shell-pink and it was beautiful. The most beautiful house she had ever seen.

Strangely, though, there was nothing about it to connect it to the man sitting opposite her. Inside everything was perfect but impersonal—

like a stage set. Surely his whole life couldn't be a performance? Not in his home?

'Why aren't you eating? Do you want something else?'

Achileas frowned at her across the table. He was dressed casually, in linen trousers and a T-shirt, but somehow that only seemed to emphasise his innate unadorned authority.

'The kitchen can make you whatever you want.'

By 'the kitchen', he meant Yiannis and Anna. Feeling a swirling rush of solidarity with the nameless behind-the-scenes staff, she immediately helped herself to yogurt. 'No, thank you, this is wonderful.'

And it was. Rich and gloriously creamy, with a hint of lemon. The tiny custard-filled pastries were delicious too.

Achileas watched her while she ate. He didn't eat, but maybe he had eaten earlier. Or maybe masters of the universe didn't eat breakfast.

As she put down her spoon he shifted back in his chair, his blue eyes calmer now.

'We might have to adjust the timeline a little, but I think it's best if we stick as closely to the truth as possible.' He took a sip of his coffee. 'That way it will all flow quite naturally between us.'

She knew he was talking about the story they would tell people—about how they'd met and fallen in love—but something in his darkly handsome face made her pulse pick up and her stomach knot as she remembered what had happened the last time it had all flowed 'naturally' between them.

'Actually, I think we should probably keep as far away from the truth as we can,' she said quietly. 'Being forced into a car by a stranger isn't usually a prelude to marriage.'

He stared at her steadily. 'Depends on the stranger.'

She felt the knot in her belly twist.

It was easier to be around him when he was angry. Safer. Cleaner. There wasn't any muddying of emotion. Her chest tightened as he leaned forward to pour some more coffee. It was even safer when he wasn't sitting so close. Because he smelled so good it made her want to breathe him in, to bottle him...

'Perhaps we could say you were rescuing me from a difficult guest,' she said, inching back in her chair.

The corners of his mouth curved very slightly. 'Like I said, we should stick as closely to the truth as possible. Maybe play around with a *Cinderella*-style narrative.'

That was a good idea. Perfect in every way, Effie thought. Except, of course, Prince Charming and Cinderella's marriage was based on love, not lies.

It took another hour before Achileas was satisfied with the start they'd made. 'Obviously we'll go over it again.' He finished his coffee. 'But we don't want to sound too scripted.'

She nodded. It was easy to see why he was so successful. He was meticulous and focused, but he also had an ability to take a step back and see the big picture. In other words, he was more than just a pretty face. And that face was more than pretty. 'Pretty' was slight and ephemeral. Achileas Kane was beautiful. Unequivocally. In a way that transcended human limitations.

'Is there a problem?'

Looking up, she found herself impaled by his disturbingly intense gaze and, horrified that he might read her thoughts—that last thought in particular—she shook her head. 'No, I was just wondering how you ended up owning this island?'

He shifted back in his chair, his fingers tapping against the handle of his coffee cup. 'The usual way,' he said finally. 'I saw it. I wanted it. I bought it.'

Her stomach clenched. Was that what had happened outside the Stanmore too?

In a way, yes. And yet at the hotel he had simply seen the maid's uniform and not the woman inside. And afterwards he had only registered the details that mattered to him. Her lack of money.

Her ability to keep her head. That was the Effie he'd seen and wanted. The Effie he had bought.

Everything else was of no interest to him.

Her pulse jerked as his phone began to vibrate against the table. He snatched it up, his lip curling like a wolf protecting its kill.

'*Wait!*' he snapped into the mouthpiece as he got to his feet. 'I have to take this, and then I have some other calls to make, so I won't be joining you for lunch, but we can finish up later.' His eyes found hers. 'Stay away from the cliffs. In fact, don't go wandering off again,' he said, in that imperious way that was as much a part of him as breathing. 'If you want to swim, use the pool.'

'I can't swim,' she said quickly. Not really… not out of her depth anyway.

He stared at her blankly, as if she had suddenly admitted to sleeping upside down in a tree. 'In that case, stay away from the pool too.' He glanced down at her face; his brow creased. 'It'll get hot this afternoon—much hotter than this—so keep out of the sun. Can't have you overheating.'

He leaned forward and she felt a wave of heat wash over her skin as he caught the brim of her hat and straightened it.

'After all, you'll be no use to me if you get sunstroke,' he added softly.

She watched him leave, her heart beating

heavily in her chest, feeling stupid. Just for a few half-seconds she had thought he cared about her as a person. But he'd just been thinking about his own agenda. And now he had upped and gone.

Only what had she expected?

That he would stay and spend time with her because...? Because what? *Because of that kiss?*

The memory rose up inside her...more than a memory. It was tactile, scorching a path through her as if it had just happened. And then she remembered that look of dark impatience on his face and she shivered inside.

Stupid, stupid Effie.

It hadn't been real. She knew that. Knew, too, that it didn't matter that she was no longer wearing a uniform. When Achileas looked at her he still saw a chambermaid. Somebody paid to make everything look perfect.

Only instead of rearranging the contents of his mini bar or turning down the sheets on his bed, she was here to turn his life into a storybook romance.

She felt a spark of defiance. This was her life too, and maybe he *was* investing in her business, but he was wrong if he thought that made her *just* an investment.

He was right about the temperature, though.

It was getting hotter. And hotter.

The house, though, was cool. There was a beautiful light breeze that fluttered through the villa, and with each tentative breath of air came that same intoxicating blend of sea spray and sunshine and herbs. So many fragrant herbs she felt almost drunk.

Did they grow wild on the island? Or was there a garden attached to the villa? Maybe later, when it got cooler, she might venture out to see, but until then…

Pulse quickening, she hurried to her room and retrieved her olfactive kit. Her fingers trembled against the wooden case. Other people had paintings or jewellery, but this was her most precious possession. It was like a genie in a lamp and a magic carpet rolled into one.

She might never have left England until yesterday, but in her tiny flat at Praed Gardens she could open this vial of cardamom and be transported to Jemaa el-Fnaa, Marrakech's main square. Unstopper the petitgrain and she was in Provence.

Only this time would be different. This time, for the first time, she wouldn't be conjuring up a fantasy but attempting to capture a real-time experience. A moment of hope and possibility.

Fresh citrus, then—to create dynamism—starting with neroli. She leaned forward, forgetting Achileas and her doubts, feeling a rush of excitement pulsing down to her fingertips.

'What's the stock trading at?'

Shifting back in his seat, Achileas stared out

of the window. Never a good sign. But then, he already knew the answer to the question. He always knew the answer to any question he asked.

All except one.

Who are you?

He'd asked Effie Price that question a week ago and he was still no closer to really knowing the answer, and now it was starting to bug him.

Normally he took pride in his ability to read people.

Take the man on the other end of the phone. Dan Ryan. His newest portfolio manager. In five years' time Dan would have upgraded his suit to a more expensive design, and as well as his college sweetheart wife he would have a mistress. There would be a couple of children. Then another affair, this time more serious, followed by a divorce and another couple of children.

It was all so predictable, but avoidable if you accepted that biology and love were essentially incompatible.

'Sixty-five dollars. When we close the deal, we could be looking at a nineteen percent bump. It's your call, of course, but I'd like to size up.' Dan's voice was quivering with testosterone.

Something pale fluttered at the edge of Achileas's vision and his gaze narrowed. It was stupid, but some part of his brain kept expecting to see Effie in that hat drifting out of view, but it was just a bird—a gull. A flicker of irritation beat a path around his body, and he frowned, his patience and interest at an end.

'Find out who's being floated as the new CEO,' he said tersely. 'Then come back to me.'

He hung up.

Dan was smart, hungry, and desperate to prove himself. But desperation made you take stupid risks. Made you fly too close to the sun.

He was suddenly gripping the phone so tightly his palms hurt. The ache in his chest felt as if he'd swallowed a boulder. Was that what was happening here? Was he flying too close to the sun? Effie was so young and untested. Could she really pull this off? And what would happen if she couldn't?

Not wanting to dwell on exactly how that made him feel, he slammed his laptop shut. He was just tense for the very obvious reason that he had put this plan together almost on a whim, and now it was in play it was hard not to look for weaknesses.

Then try harder, he told himself firmly.

Standing up, he twisted his neck from side to side, rolling his shoulders. Maybe he would take that swim now. Or, better still, he could work off his tension on the punchbag.

As he walked through the cool interior of the villa, he remembered Effie asking him how he had ended up buying the island. He had condensed his answer into three short sentences, but it had actually been a long and conflicted process.

His mouth twisted. An internally conflicted process. The same old push-me-pull-you battle that always happened whenever he confronted his Greek heritage.

But there had been something about the location of the island—near the mainland, but not so close that he had to acknowledge his father's proximity—and he had felt a curious affinity with the incongruously pink neoclassical house with a chequered past.

What the—?

He came to an abrupt halt. He was supposed to be heading towards the gym. But apparently that particular memo hadn't reached his legs. Why else would he be standing in the doorway to the sitting room, staring as though hypnotised by the sight of Effie Price's downturned and hatless head?

The waft of her scent made his chest feel suddenly too tight for his ribcage and he gritted his teeth. She was leaning over one of the low coffee tables. Beside her was a hinged wooden box, a bit like a paintbox. It was open. But instead of paints it held rows of glass vials filled with clear liquid.

'What are you doing?'

He knew his voice was unnecessarily harsh from the way her face jerked up to meet his, but he didn't care. In fact, he hoped it would encourage her to keep her distance. And remind her who was in charge.

'I was just playing around with some oils.'

His eyes dropped to the neat wooden case and despite himself he realised he was interested. A lot more interested than he had been earlier, talking to Dan Ryan.

'Playing to what end?' he found himself asking.

There was a tiny fluttering pause as her brown eyes rested on his face, composed but wary. 'I'm trying to create a fragrance.'

Of course she was. Probably another wicked concoction that would make his head spin like a carousel.

'And how do you do that?'

This time the pause that followed his question seemed to stretch through the open French windows to the horizon.

'It's a process,' she said at last. 'I start with an idea of the end scent, and then I have to think about what raw materials might produce that effect. In this case, I want to create something that is not too heavy. I want it to come and go like the lightest of breezes. But I still want it to stop you in your tracks.'

Effie was speaking quietly but he could hear her excitement, her passion. Glancing down, he noted both her flushed cheeks and the press of her nipples against the fabric of her dress, and he felt his body tighten with a different excitement as he remembered how she had turned to flame in his arms.

Had that been a one-off? Did making perfume normally absorb all her passion? What if some of that passion escaped again?

It was only then that he realised Effie was staring up at him, and that he had no idea how much time had passed since she'd started speaking.

'...that's the plan...' Her voice trailed off and she began to pick up the vials and slot them back in the case. 'Anyway, did you want to go over what we talked about this morning?'

He shook his head. 'No, I want to know how you make a fragrance that comes and goes but stops you in your tracks.' Actually, it was simpler even than that. He just wanted her to keep talking. 'I need to know,' he added quickly. 'I mean, I would know something about your job if this was a real relationship.'

She stared at him as if considering the logic of his words. 'I suppose that's true.' Her small white teeth chewed at her lip. 'Well, I started with neroli...but it wasn't vivacious enough.' Picking up one of the vials, she squeezed a drop of oil onto one of the thin strips of card and waved it in front of her face. 'This works better. It's bergamot. It's one of my favourites because it's the most multifaceted of all the citrus materials.'

Leaning forward, he took the blotting paper

from her hand. Her fingers brushed against his and he felt that phosphorus flare of desire as her eyes jerked up to his face at the whisper of contact.

He breathed in cautiously. 'Oranges? But spicier?'

She nodded. 'There's a woody aspect which will work well with the base notes I have in mind.'

He watched her run her hand over the vials.

'Now, because bergamot can be a little warm, I want to add clarity and brightness with pink pepper.'

It was oddly relaxing, watching her open the bottles and add tiny drops of pepper, then lime and lavender. In fact, he felt calmer than he had in weeks.

'Is that it?' he asked.

'I wish.'

She shook her head, and then suddenly he forgot all about the perfume and the deal he'd made with her, and even about the ache in his chest, because she smiled a smile of such sweetness that everything he'd thought he knew and cared about was erased. It was a smile that changed her face, added light and colour and something indefinable, so that he found himself smiling back at her.

'This is just the starting point,' she said. 'Like the rough sketch of a dress you want to make.

From here, I'll have to keep playing with different oils to build the composition, and then I'll have to add the alcohol.'

He held her gaze. 'How do you remember it all?'

She lifted up a notebook—the cheap kind with a cardboard cover. 'I take notes. Why don't you try some of the samples while I get this down on paper? See if you can work out what they are. Then maybe you can try mixing some oils.'

In other words, he should play quietly.

Watching her pick up a pen, he felt an odd mix of outrage and admiration. He hadn't been told what to do since he was a child. In business, most people fell over themselves to attract his attention and hold it. It was the same with women.

But not this woman. She had that same purity of focus that he'd had at her age.

Unnerved by the idea that he and Effie had something in common other than the deal they had made, he picked up one of the vials at random and opened it. It was numbered, not named, but he knew immediately that it was lemon.

Feeling pleased, he picked another. That was harder. It was spicy. Like Christmas. Cinnamon? Cloves? He frowned and held up a third to his nose, breathed—

His heartbeat stumbled, then stopped. He felt his face dissolve with shock.

He was back in England. It was a cold, wet

day, and he was cold, and his clothes were wet, and he ached everywhere—but especially in his chest. He felt desperate and wretched and lonely, winded by loneliness...

With an effort, he pulled his face from the black velvet gravity inside the open bottle and placed it down with extravagant care. 'What is this?'

Effie glanced sideways at the bottle. 'That's a synthetic for oakmoss. The original was—'

She looked up and frowned. She was talking to herself. Achileas was gone.

CHAPTER FIVE

'LET'S TAKE COFFEE out on the deck.'

Pushing back his chair, Achileas got to his feet and strode away from the terrace to where a group of cream linen sofas sat at elegant right angles. Behind them the Aegean was dark and shiny like spilt ink, except where the feathery evening sunlight danced across the surface like falling stars.

Effie watched him drop down onto the furthest sofa. It had been a long, disconcerting, and exhausting day, and she wasn't sure that she wanted to be out here alone with this baffling, mercurial man who made her say and feel stupid things.

Not that she could decline his invitation because he hadn't actually invited her. Although no doubt his autocratic suggestion passed for an invitation among men of his power and wealth.

After he'd absented himself from lunch, she had half wondered if he would bother dining with her, but when she'd stepped outside into the warm evening air at exactly eight o'clock, he'd been standing at the edge of the terrace, his gaze fixed on something in the distance. Even when he had joined her at the table his gaze had returned often to the endless sea.

He was either distracted or bored or both. And, despite the meal being a masterclass of flavour combinations, he'd barely eaten. Just pushed the food around the plate as if that bored him too.

'Thank you, that was delicious,' she said now, as Demy the housekeeper appeared and began to quietly clear the table. 'Could you thank Yiannis for me?'

Achileas's staff had been lined up outside the house when they'd arrived, but she had been too tired to take in his terse rollcall of names and she had asked Demy to introduce her. There were some things she was willing to fake, but for this arrangement to work she needed to be true to herself—and that meant treating people with respect.

Even if it made things bumpy between her and Achileas.

A current of unease snaked across her skin. So far each time she had been herself things had got more than 'bumpy' between them.

She thought back to his abrupt exit earlier.

Bumpy and baffling.

And probably that wasn't going to change any time soon, given that they had nothing in common aside from an upcoming marriage of convenience. They were just two strangers who had met a little over a week ago, living under the same roof.

Effie glanced over to where Achileas was sitting, her breathing suddenly unsteady.

Except he wasn't a complete stranger to her. In fact, the more she spent time with him, the more he reminded her of her father.

Bill had moods too.

Sometimes he'd been great company. As a child she could remember watching him at a wedding. People were gathered around him and bursts of laughter had erupted as he'd told a joke or a funny story, and she had been proud of him, her handsome, charming dad.

Other days he was sullen and monosyllabic. He threw things at the wall when the bets he'd made at the bookies that day had gone sideways. And sometimes he'd just get up from eating or watching TV and disappear without a word or a backward glance. Often, he would be gone for days.

In those moments she had wanted to cry. Wanted a different father. One who didn't stay up all night playing poker in the back room of some pub. One who knew when to stop. But Bill hadn't wanted to stop. He hadn't been able to. Gambling had been his life. Everything else—everyone else—had bored him.

Including her.

So why should Achilleas find her any less boring? She had seen the calibre of woman he usually dated and discarded. Even if she had been his type why would he be interested in her? He barely knew her.

And yet earlier today, when they had talked about the process of making a perfume, she had felt as if they had known one another not for days but for the whole of her life.

In those few moments he had seemed to change before her eyes. For the first time since they'd met the tension and the impatience that were as much a part of him as the stubble shadowing the curve of his jaw had seemed to lift. In those few moments she had glimpsed a different man.

A less guarded man.

A man not moving purposefully forward but happy to wait, to listen, to watch, to share.

A man with a smile that could make the sun melt. A smile that was almost as devastating as his kiss.

She blanked her mind. Or that was what she thought she was doing. But, heart thumping, she replayed that moment when he'd put the vial of oakmoss on the table and left without a word.

Oakmoss, or *mousse de chêne* as it was also known, belonged to the chypre family. It was actually a lichen which grew on oaks throughout

Europe and North Africa. It had a unique scent. Both earthy and woody, with hints of musk, it was really not like anything else in the perfumer's 'palette'.

The one snag was that it had been blacklisted as a potential irritant, so its use had been restricted, forcing perfumers to play around with other ingredients like patchouli, or synthetic imitations of oakmoss.

It had been a long and frustrating process, she knew, to blend a synthetic that matched the original. But it needed to be done. Not only did oakmoss give a scent a longer life on the skin, but it was also widely used to anchor volatile notes in a fragrance.

She shivered. If only there was a scent that could anchor Achileas's volatile notes. But even with around two hundred essential oils and one thousand five hundred synthetic materials to choose from, she wasn't confident she could do that.

Getting to her feet, she made her way over to where he was sitting just as Demy arrived with a tray of coffee and petit fours.

'Just leave it,' he said tersely, flicking the housekeeper away with his hand. Effie gave Demy a small, tight smile and sat down on the sofa opposite him.

'I was thinking,' he said, stretching out his

legs, 'about how to explain our getting from that first meeting to me asking you out...'

Effie frowned. 'But you wouldn't have asked me out.'

There was a short pulsing silence as the distance between them seemed to shrink and fill with a familiar dark impatience—the same dark impatience with which he'd dismissed Demy. It was always there, as if something was constantly chafing him. Only how could that be? He was wealthy and powerful. If that were true, he would simply snap his fingers and make it go away.

'You're not suggesting you would have asked me?' Eyes narrowing, he held her gaze as she shook her head slowly. 'Then what? Because I thought we agreed this would be a Cinderella story.' His lip curled. 'Surely you know how that works? It is, after all, a tale as old as time.'

'That's the wrong fairy tale,' she corrected him quietly.

Now the corners of his mouth twisted in what would probably be the beginning of a smile with anyone else. But this was Achileas, and it could just as easily be a scowl or a frown.

It was a scowl.

'Is there a difference? It's all happy ever after in the end.'

He shifted back against the sofa cushion, and when he spoke again, she could hear the harnessed tension in his voice. 'My point is that Cinderella is asked out by the Prince. In case you're having trouble following the conversation, in this scenario that's me.'

She felt her own flicker of impatience. 'He thinks she's a princess when he dances with her at the ball. In this scenario, obviously I'm not a princess. I'm Housekeeping,' she said pointedly.

There was another silence, longer this time, and thickly solid like the blanketing silence that followed a heavy fall of snow, expanding and thickening around her so that she could no longer hear the sound of the waves.

He shrugged. 'So, I saw past the uniform.'

His blue gaze hurt where it rested on her face. 'Isn't that love?'

The cynicism in his voice hurt even more than his gaze.

How could he be so jaded? So dismissive?

She thought about her mum, always hopeful, always wanting to believe that this time would be different. And her father too, tearfully begging for another chance. Both of them buying into the dream of love over and over again, even though theirs was damaged beyond repair.

Yet here was Achileas, the product of a forty-year happy marriage, with a sneer in his voice.

'I thought we'd agreed to stick as closely to the truth as possible,' she said quietly. 'In that case, we should say you dropped off my folder and that should be the end of it. After that we can

get creative, but wherever we say we met next
has to be somewhere away from the hotel. Somewhere random. Somewhere nobody would know
either of us. Where I'm not a maid and you're
not…' she hesitated, her eyes drifting over his
astonishingly beautiful, unforgettable face '…
you're not you.'

She blinked as Achileas leaned forward, his
muscular shoulders bunching beneath his T-shirt.
For a moment she thought that he would dismiss
her with one of those careless gestures he seemed
to have at his fingertips. Instead, he picked up
the coffee pot and poured out two cups.

Jaw tightening, Achileas watched Effie take her
cup with a hand that trembled ever so slightly.

But that was Effie Price all over. She didn't
scream or shout or throw things, only somehow
that only made her quiver of resistance more
seismic.

She had no reason to be angry, he thought irritably.

Okay, he was brusque with his staff, and
maybe that touched a nerve with her, but it wasn't
as if he was expecting *her* to lift a finger. All
she had to do was learn her lines and lie in the
sun. And if she thought he was about to modify
his behaviour, then she could think again. She'd
known who he was before she signed on the dot-
ted line, and he had been straight with her.

Well, to a point.

Clearly, he couldn't tell her the whole truth, and nor did he want to. There was no need for Effie, of all people, to know that Andreas had only recently reached out to him. Or that his father's acceptance came with conditions. That was between him and Andreas and way over Effie's paygrade.

But some truths would have to be shared. She was going to find out that his mother and father were not a couple who had been married for forty years, and he was planning on telling her when he was ready.

So, yes, he had been and would be straight with her. But Effie—

He let out a breath he hadn't realised he was holding and felt his temper rise. This was her doing. She was the reason he couldn't breathe. It was bad enough that her teasing scent seemed to mark every surface...then she had to go and start mixing her potions in his sitting room.

The memory of holding that vial up to his nose pulsed in his head, bright like a neon sign, hurting the insides of his eyes.

He'd had to leave. He hadn't been able to stand there with that awful, raging thing scrabbling inside him and he still wasn't sure what had happened. One minute he had been inhaling the scent of oranges in an oasis of calm, the next—

His stomach clenched. Maybe that was why

he had reacted so strongly. It was rare for him to feel so at peace, so at one with himself. In fact, he couldn't recall ever feeling like that.

Not even when he was a child.

Particularly not when he was a child.

Then again, while Effie might be the very definition of ordinary, with her brown hair and brown eyes and sensible clothes, this situation was exceptional. How could it not be? He was a man who didn't believe in love or matrimony, pretending to be in love with a woman he had met a week ago. A woman he was planning to marry, all so that he could punish one man. The father who had walked out of his life before he was even born.

He was turning himself inside out. Turning into a stranger.

Surely that, not this woman or some random scent, was the reason he was so on edge. But now was not the time to analyse that.

'Doesn't sound too hard,' he said, watching the sun's slow burnished descent into the sea. 'My free time is limited but it happens. I'm sure if we "get creative" we can come up with a solution.'

Her light brown eyes fixed on his face. 'I think you and I have very different definitions of that word.'

'Which one? Creative?' Leaning forward, he nudged the coffee cup towards her. 'Hard?'

Watching the pulse twitch at the base of her

throat, he shifted back in his seat, conscious suddenly of the hammering of his heart.

She lifted her chin, held his gaze. 'It's complicated. You and I would never normally cross paths so it needs to be somewhere we could have met by chance, and yet it needs not to have been by chance at all, because it was a place we had in common all the time only without realising. Does that make sense?'

It did. He couldn't have put it better himself. In fact, he hadn't.

He held her gaze, torn between curiosity and admiration. 'Where do you have in mind?'

She sat up a little straighter, tilting her face the better to look at him. He knew there was no logical reason for it, and yet he still couldn't stop the tiny lick of flame as he caught sight of the pale underside of her throat.

'I was thinking of a garden or a gallery, depending on what you like doing in your free time.'

As she leaned forward to pick up her coffee her scent whipped at his senses, so that he had to press his body back into the seat to stop himself from climbing over the small glass-topped table and pulling her against him as he had in the car.

Taking a shallow breath, he let his gaze cruise casually over her small, tense body. 'I'm not sure either would be entirely suitable for what I like doing in my free time.'

She stared at him, the faintest flush of pink colouring her cheeks. 'How about a funfair, then?'

His pulse stumbled. He had wanted to get under her skin as her scent was getting under his, but instead he felt the slight hoarseness in her voice in all the wrong places. 'Why a funfair?'

'We could have gone on the dodgems. Bumped into one another intentionally for once.'

He laughed. Because it was funny. *She* was funny. And he was surprised to find that his anger and resentment of moments earlier was, like the sun, fading fast.

'We might just have done that,' he said slowly.

He couldn't remember the last time he had gone to a funfair. In fact, he couldn't remember 'fun' ever being part of his vocabulary. When he was a child, he'd worked and eaten and slept. As an adult, that list had lengthened to include working out and hooking up with women for a different kind of workout. But somehow fun—easy, lazy, meandering fun—had never played a part in his life.

There was always something driving him forward, a restlessness that haunted him, snapped at his heels. Even now, when he didn't need to work, when he could arguably just kick back and relax, he couldn't stop.

Glancing over at Effie's small, pale face, he felt his pulse slow. He couldn't remember the last time he had laughed with a woman either.

Perhaps he never had. Laughter meant having the kind of intimacy that slowed things down, and he had never wanted to take things slowly. If he did that he might have to stop and think about who he was. And, more importantly, who he wasn't.

He cleared his throat. 'Practically speaking, though, a garden or gallery would be more believable. And I'm not really into gardens so…'

A memory, long buried, shuffled from the wings into the spotlight. A school trip, and then later, when he'd been old enough to go alone, furtive visits by himself.

'What about the British Museum?'

They both spoke at once.

Effie frowned up at him, her brown eyes tangling with his for a second, and then the corners of her mouth fluttered upwards into another of those mesmerizingly sweet smiles that made his heart beat faster.

No, they weren't brown, he thought with a twitch of surprise. They were amber…like the colour of iced tea. Her hair wasn't just brown either. There were strands of gold and red too, like autumn leaves spinning through pale sunlight.

'You like the British Museum?' he asked.

'It's one of my favourite places in the world. Not that I've seen much of the world.' Her eyelashes fluttered like moths around a lamp. 'I used to go there when I had a split shift. They have the most amazing glass perfume bottles from Ancient Egypt and Greece. Some of them are shaped like animals and others are incredibly simple, but beautiful, like a teardrop.'

Suddenly he couldn't quite catch his breath. She was moved by the memory. He could feel how important it was to her. Her excitement caught fire in him, too, and then out of nowhere he had the strangest feeling...almost like regret.

Regret that this wasn't real—that it never could be real for him. That he would never be able to make it real for her.

He shook off the thought. 'The British Museum it is, then.'

The look on her face altered, the smile flattening as if she realised that she had revealed more than she had intended.

'I think that would work, but...' she hesitated '...if you've changed your mind about all this, then it's not too late to say so.'

The sun had moved lower now, and the light was starting to fade. He felt a momentary chill. 'I haven't changed my mind.'

Straightening up, he drew back his legs as if to distance himself from that possibility. Effie didn't speak for a moment, and he frowned, impatient suddenly, again.

'Are you saying you have? Because—'

'I'm not saying that.' She shook her head, her brown eyes finding his. 'It's just that it's all happened very quickly, and earlier I thought you seemed…it seemed…'

He watched it all going through her head: those few moments of unscripted easiness between them, his abrupt departure, her struggle to understand. But for her to understand he would need to explain everything that had happened, and he couldn't put that into words. He didn't have the words.

He shrugged. 'It's just strange, sharing my space. I don't do that.'

The doubt faded a little from her face. 'It is strange,' she said at last. 'I haven't shared my space either, since—'

She stumbled over the word, and he felt a sting against his skin—fine, like a paper cut. *Since Sam.* That was what she had been about to say… only she couldn't say it.

'When did he move out?' he asked.

Now her gaze was on him again, wide-eyed, bewildered.

'Who?'

'Your boyfriend. Sam.' For some reason, that sentence was a lot harder to say out loud than it had been in his head. 'The one who painted you.'

The one you're still in love with, he almost added.

For a moment she didn't reply. She just stared at him as if she was trying to put into words what she was feeling. Then, 'Sam's not my boyfriend. She's not even a boy.'

Now it was his turn to stare. His eyes locked with hers as he replayed that moment in her flat when she had melted into him, the soft touch of her mouth and that shimmering charged heat that danced over his skin. Had that been an illusion on his part? An experiment on hers?

'Are you saying—?'

'No.' She was shaking her head. 'No. Sam's my mum.'

But of course she was. And the relief he was feeling was completely understandable. The situation was already complicated enough as it was. 'Why didn't you say that at the time?'

'I panicked. I suppose I thought it wouldn't matter, because you were just returning my folder, but now it does matter.' Her pupils flared. 'I don't like telling lies. It's wrong and it always ends up hurting someone.'

Stung by the unspoken accusation in that sentence, he said nothing, just let the silence stretch out and swallow up the memory of her words. 'In that case,' he said at last, 'I wonder why you've agreed to this. Actually, you don't need to explain.' His body tensed as he realised he already knew and irrationally hated the answer. 'I'm guessing the money has helped overcome your normal scruples.'

'It isn't like that.' Effie stared at Achileas, feeling the ripple of his anger move through her and beyond to the darkening sky, feeling her own anger rising in her throat. 'You're trying to make me feel guilty about a situation that *you* engineered,' she said, as calmly as she could.

Except she did feel a kind of shame for the lies she had already told and the lies she was going to have to keep telling.

'Is that so?' he said, mildly enough, but there was a dark gleam in his blue eyes like a shark's fin cutting through the surface of the waves.

She felt her breath catch. 'Yes, it is. I do feel bad about lying to people. And, yes, I am marrying you for the money, because that's what we agreed. But it's not the only reason. If you were just performing this charade out of self-interest I wouldn't have agreed for any amount of money.'

Was that true? She quickly searched her soul, panicked suddenly that she had become by stealth the kind of person she most feared becoming. Someone who lied not just to other people but to themselves.

But it was true. She couldn't have agreed to lie to Achileas's father for some scurrilous, self-serving motive any more than she could have burgled his home.

'You're lying to make your father happy. You're trying to give him what he wants the only way you can. That's why I'm here. Because you're trying to be a good son.'

And she understood that impulse. She would have done anything for her father. She still would. Not that any kind of intervention would work now. And maybe that was why, deep down, she had agreed to this crazy fake marriage. She might not be able to help Bill, but she could help Achileas make his father happy.

'It's all I've ever wanted.' His blue gaze rested on her face, dark now in the fading light. 'But I can see that might not have been immediately obvious at our first meeting.'

Their first meeting. A shocking point of contact like a fork of lightning. His iron grip on her arm. Her caught breath and that uncontrollable shiver of longing that had left her dizzy and aching.

Pushing away the memory, she nodded. The movement seemed to unlock her rigid body and gratefully she stood up. 'It's been a long day, so I think I might turn in—'

She spun round, intending to walk away.

'Why did you panic?'

Her feet stuttered to a halt, her head spinning madly at the sudden shift in conversation. Turning, she felt her stomach knot as she saw that Achileas had got to his feet and was staring at her, his gaze boring into her so that suddenly she wanted to turn and run. But her body was rooted to the stone terrace as if she was part of it.

'Earlier? You said that was why you lied about who Sam was.' He took a step closer. 'You said you panicked.'

Looking up into his beautiful face, she felt a jolt. The skin over his cheeks was pulled taut, like a fitted sheet over a too-big mattress. Only it was not with anger or impatience, but some other emotion that she couldn't name.

'You said you weren't scared of me.'

'I'm not.' She spoke without hesitation. She wasn't. Not in the way he meant, anyway, she thought a moment later. Only how could she put into words what she had felt? Why she had felt it.

'Then why panic?'

She stared at his lush mouth, feeling utterly off balance, as if she was a pendulum, swinging between a need to keep her personal life hidden from him and a need to lay it bare.

'I wasn't expecting you. You just turned up on my doorstep uninvited. And, in case you've forgotten, the last time we'd met you'd bundled me off the street into your car.'

'So you were scared.'

The knot in her stomach tightened. His voice had a way of demanding, *commanding* answers, and she knew he wouldn't stop until his questions were satisfied.

Inching backwards, away from the force field intensity of his will, she shook her head. 'Not scared. I just didn't want to give anything of myself away. I suppose I didn't want you to know that I'd never had a boyfriend. Never done anything…'

Her voice trailed off, but she didn't need to finish the sentence.

A muscle worked in his jaw. 'By "never done anything", you mean you're a virgin?'

Suddenly the silence was thick enough to slice. He was staring at her as if she had announced she was a mermaid. Was it that unusual? Surely she couldn't be the only virgin he had met in his life?

She lifted her chin. 'Yes, that is what I mean. And I'm perfectly fine with that,' she said, trying desperately not to sound as breathless as she felt.

Achileas didn't move a muscle, but something shifted. A slight movement in the air. A change to the light as if she had inadvertently touched a dimmer switch.

'So why did you kiss me, then?'

Her pulse darted like a startled bird. She had been pretending all day that it didn't exist. Now, though, the silken, shimmering thread that was between them pulled taut with an audible snap. His eyes were fixed on her face, and she knew that he could see the faint tremor beneath her skin. The flush across her cheeks.

'I didn't kiss you,' she managed at last. 'You kissed me.'

The last rays of sun glimmered around his face like flames.

'I kissed you first,' he said softly.

His gaze narrowed in on hers in a way that made her breath go shallow.

'But you still kissed me.'

She had bundled that moment into the suitcase with all her clothes, relieved not to have to think about it. Only no secret ever stayed secret for long. As the daughter of a gambler, she should know that better than anyone.

She swallowed. Every single nerve in her body was quivering on high alert. 'I didn't know it could feel like that. That's why I panicked. I wasn't expecting to feel, to want—'

His beautiful, astonishing mouth curved into a question. 'To want what, Effie?'

At some point they had drifted closer—too close. Close enough to touch. Heart hammering, she looked past him at the dark blue sea. But that was a mistake because it was like looking straight into Achileas's eyes, and suddenly they were there, back at the edge of the cliffs, only this time he wasn't stopping her falling.

'This…' she said hoarsely. And, standing on tiptoe, she tilted her mouth and kissed him.

There was a moment when he tensed, and panic of a different kind fluttered in her throat.

Perhaps her memories of that first kiss had been wrong—a feverish dream conjured up by the shock of his beauty and the scent of his skin. But then his hand wrapped around her waist, and he took her kiss as if he had been waiting for it his whole life. As if she was already his.

And it was nothing like that first kiss. That had been a sensual exploration, a deliberate provocation designed to stir her, to make her unravel. This was rawer, hungrier, as if he was as out of control as she was.

Heat rolled through her. Pinpricks of light exploded behind her eyes as his mouth moved over hers. And then his tongue parted her lips, and she tasted the dark bite of coffee and desire. Knotting her fists into his shirt, she pulled him closer, kissing him back.

Breathing unsteadily, he pulled her against him. She felt the hard muscles of his body and, harder still, the press of his erection against the soft flesh of her thighs. Hunger flooded through her veins like a levee breaking as he groaned against her mouth, and then he was kissing her neck, licking a path to the bare skin of her shoulder, and her legs were shaking so badly that she couldn't stand.

They stumbled backwards together onto the sofa, her hands clutching at his shoulders as he pulled her hair free of its band, sliding his fingers through her hair, holding her captive. Her body was softening. The heat of his mouth, his hands, moulding her, changing her, making her want to know more, to feel more—to be his.

With a small sound she arched into him, her fingers pulling clumsily at his shirt. He shifted above her, the hard planes of his chest crushing her breasts, making them ache, making the nipples tighten painfully, and she gasped.

He jerked backwards as if stung and she reached up to him, stung herself by the abrupt withdrawal of his body.

'Stop.' His hands dropped to her waist, and he held her down. 'Effie, stop.'

His breath was hot and uneven, just as hers was. She gazed up at him, her heart pounding, her body twitching with longing, need flickering over her skin like flames across an oil slick.

'What is it?'

'You should go.'

Her face felt as if it was burning. 'I thought—'

'Then you thought wrong. Your first time should be with someone who cares about you. Not someone who's paying you.' He stared down at her, his face hard, hostile. 'You need to go to bed. On your own.'

He took a step backwards, as if he was fighting for control. Or expecting her to drag him with her.

'I said go,' he snapped as she stared up at him dazedly.

And, cheeks burning, she got to her feet and went.

CHAPTER SIX

IT WAS EARLY.

Walking swiftly, Effie glanced sideways across the smooth water, lavender-coloured in the dawn light, to where the sun was inching up past the horizon. It was pale yellow and tinged on the underside with blue.

Calm, unshakeable, untroubled.

Turning away from the sea, she trembled. If only she could change places with the sun.

She had watched the sky lighten from her window and finally, when she'd been able to bear it no more, she got up and dressed and walked away from the silent villa.

She had no idea where she was going. No preset destination in mind. She just needed to move and keep moving.

Her sandalled feet slipped sideways and, reaching out, she rested her hand against an outcrop of lead-coloured rock.

She felt as if she hadn't slept at all. She'd stared into the darkness, her body rigid like a block of wood, her eyes dry and scratchy. Of course, she had fallen asleep, but it had been a short respite from her tumultuous thoughts. Now she was awake, and if anything, she felt worse now than last night, when she'd fled from the terrace and Achileas's single-word rejection.

Her pulse beat in time to the distant ebb and flow of the waves. In the darkness, her shock and shame had been her own, but now, with the sun rising, she was going to have to face him. It was nearly seven hours since she had made a complete and utter fool of herself by kissing Achileas beneath the setting sun, but it might as well have been seven seconds.

She could remember it exactly. Not just a frame-by-frame replay of what had happened but of how it had felt. The heaviness of her breasts and that flower of heat blossoming between her thighs. Soft, quivering, insistent...

Her fingers shook as they had when she had touched the hard muscles of his chest and arms, and she breathed out shakily. Leaning forward, she pressed her hot forehead against the coolness of the rock. But it couldn't douse the heat beneath her skin.

She swallowed past the lump in her throat, unsure if the tears she was holding back were down to panic at what she had done or shame at her stupidity. Both, probably, although shame might have it in a photo finish.

Thinking back to the moment when Achileas had broken away from her, she rested her hand on the place in her stomach where she had felt that treacherous melting. Why had she done it? She had known that kiss they'd shared in her flat hadn't been anything more than a means to prove a point, only for some reason she had forgotten that fact. She had forgotten everything. Not just where they were and why they were there, but who they were.

Who she was.

Until Achileas had reminded her.

At the unguarded memory her eyes began to sting.

He had been blunt at first, but not unkind. Only her head had still been spinning with the drugging intensity of his hard mouth on hers and so she had just stood there. And then he'd snapped at her. Like an impatient grown-up dispatching a child who had tried to stay up after her bedtime.

Her cheeks burned at the memory. As if a man of Achileas's experience would be remotely interested in *her*. She had seen the women he dated—or one of them, anyway—and Tamara was sexy and sophisticated, not some clueless virgin.

And just because she was ready to be changed, it didn't mean he felt the same way.

Her one and only consolation out of the whole

horrific mess was that Achileas was unlikely to bring it up so she wouldn't have to either. But she needed to keep replaying it inside her head until she could think about it calmly. And without her hands shaking.

It was getting sandier underfoot. Soaring dunes rose on either side of her and the path curved to the right.

She stopped short.

In front of her was a beach—a lagoon.

A perfect crescent of white ribbed sand curving in an arc around the clearest blue water she had ever seen.

It was empty, the air magically still, the sound of the waves gentle. Like a sigh, almost, or the soft intake of breath. She stared down at it, her mind emptied, all her disquiet and discomfort miraculously soothed. If she closed her eyes, it would be like when she was little, when she would climb into bed with her mum and listen to her sleep...

There was a splash and she breathed in sharply—only her eyes didn't shut. In fact, they almost popped out of her head.

She had been wrong. The beach wasn't empty.

A man was swimming, his muscular shoulders cutting through the waves with smooth, strong, rhythmic strokes like the prow of a ship.

She watched enviously, wishing she could swim with the same effortless grace. Abruptly he stopped moving beneath the water, juddering to a halt, and her breathing jerked as a head broke the surface and Achileas smoothed a hand over his face.

A ripple of panic washed over her, and then another of guilt. She shouldn't be here, spying on him. It was wrong on so many levels. Only she didn't dare move in case he spotted her. Panic replaced guilt. The thought of him emerging from the water and striding towards her like some Greek sea god, only in swim-shorts instead of some artfully draped robe, made it suddenly impossible for her to take a breath.

Hopefully he would start swimming again in a moment, and then she could retreat unobserved.

But he didn't start swimming. Instead, he just trod water with his face tilted up towards the lightening sky, as if he was communing with a higher power.

Was that why he was here?

She felt something stir inside her. There was certainly something different about him. He looked exhilarated. Freer. Lighter. Only not in the sense of being weightless—more as if a burden had been lifted from those muscular shoulders.

But before she had a chance to pursue that train of thought Achileas stood up and began wading towards the beach. She caught the gleam of light on wet skin, and then her heartbeat began stampeding like a herd of wild horses. She had been wrong again. Achileas wasn't wearing swim-shorts: he was naked. And whatever his body had felt like through his clothes, it looked a thousand times better, she thought on a rush of air.

Her skin was suddenly on fire. Now she really shouldn't be looking. But she couldn't tear her gaze away. Instead, she stared down at him, open-mouthed.

He was, hands-down, the most shockingly perfect specimen of maleness she had ever seen. A mesmerising mix of flawless sleek skin and golden muscle. She watched, hypnotised, as drops of sea water trickled down his contoured chest, over the light smattering of dark hair that arrowed down to the line that bisected his abs, then lower still to...to—

The word seemed to fill her mouth, so that suddenly it was impossible to swallow, and she dragged her gaze upwards, shock fluttering in her throat—and something else. Something sharp and persistent like thirst. Only not thirst.

As if sensing her gaze, Achileas turned, and she felt the blue of his eyes like twin gas rings. Naked flame burned her skin and she stumbled backwards. Had he seen her? *Possibly.* Should she show herself? Her pulse catapulted. *Absolutely not.*

She inched her way back up the path and then,

once she was sure there was no chance of him catching sight of her, she turned towards the villa and ran.

Her bedroom would be quiet and still. *Safe*.

Closing the door behind her, she sat down on the bed. This had to stop. And it would. She was just adjusting to living with someone again. Living with Achileas. That was all it was. That and the fact that only a short time ago she had woken every morning in her small flat with nothing more than a clumsy kiss at a party to fuel her imagination.

Her nipples tightened and she felt a thread of heat cutting through her like a freshly forged blade. She'd always had a vivid imagination. Now she had plenty of fuel for it. Too much, in fact. And none of it relevant to her arrangement with Achileas.

She glanced over at her phone. It was where she had left it on the bedside table. Picking it up, she saw that there was a message from her mum.

Have the most wonderful holiday. I can't wait to see the photos.

Picturing Sam carefully selecting each letter as she typed out her message, Effie felt her eyes burn. She loved her mum every bit as much as Achileas loved his father, and that was the reason she was here. *Not sex*—and particularly not sex with him. After all, as he'd said, her first time should be with someone who cared about her.

As she'd expected, Achileas made no mention of the night before when they met at breakfast. In fact, he behaved exactly as he had done the previous morning. As if it hadn't happened. Or he had forgotten it.

She knew she should be grateful, and she was. But it still hurt, knowing he could do that.

She made herself concentrate on spooning yoghurt into her mouth.

'I thought we might go out to lunch today.'

She glanced up, her heart lurching. 'What do you mean?' Surely he wasn't suggesting that they go public yet? It was too soon.

Not taking his eyes off her face, he raised a dark eyebrow. 'It's a meal in the middle of the day. It comes between breakfast and dinner. And by "out" I mean at a restaurant,' he said, his voice dropping a notch in a way that made her skin prickle with warning.

It wasn't a suggestion.

Her body tensed. She was already feeling fragile after last night, and she was guessing Achileas's choice of restaurant wouldn't be some small, discreet side-street taverna.

'Don't you think we should wait a little?' she said stiffly. 'I mean, we haven't really got our story straight.'

She felt a flutter of vertigo as he shifted forward, and there was a moment when it would have been so, so easy to tip herself into his clear blue eyes, but then he shrugged, dismissing her remark with a careless lift of his broad shoulders.

'Oh, I think we both know where we stand on the essential details.'

He sat back in his chair, motioning with his hand in that imperious way of his, and she watched in silence as Demy instantly appeared at his elbow with a fresh pot of coffee.

'Besides,' he said when finally, the housekeeper left them alone, 'what we do here, when we're alone, is of no consequence.'

Her spoon scraped against her empty bowl, and she quickly put it down. That told her, she thought, fighting a betraying flush of colour as he let his gaze drift dismissively past her to the Aegean.

'It can't be validated. For that to happen we need to be seen together. As a couple. Help people leap to the right conclusion.'

A couple.

Shaken by his words, she stared at him mutely. So, this was it: this was the reality of what she had agreed to back in London. Only she wasn't sure she was ready. Wasn't sure she would ever be ready.

'And how do we do that?' she asked.

His gaze narrowed across the table. 'The usual way.'

Remembering the last time he had used those words, she turned her head slightly. But she could only look away for so long and, folding her hands out of sight under the table in case they trembled, she met his gaze.

He stared back at her steadily, and she couldn't stop herself from devouring his hard, arrogant beauty. The high sweep of his cheekbones, his straight nose…and that mouth. His beautiful sensual mouth that she knew could curl into a smile no mortal woman could resist…

But he wasn't smiling now. 'We'll take the launch over to one of the other islands. We can have a look at some temples…do some shopping. Then grab some lunch.'

He made it sound so easy. Probably it would be for him. But for her…?

She felt her pulse pick up. She knew how couples behaved. London was full of them, walking hand in hand, their eyes meshed, their bodies no more than a hair's breadth apart. Would Achileas hold her hand? Would he pull her against him as they walked? Press his mouth against hers, claiming her for all to see?

Her mind shrank back from the idea even as her body responded with a burst of shimmering electric heat that she was terrified he might sense.

She squared her shoulders. 'I don't think I have anything to wear.'

Now he smiled. It pressed against her skin like hot metal.

'I thought you might say that.' He leaned back in his seat, his astonishing blue eyes locking onto hers so forcefully that she felt as if a tide had rushed in and rolled over her, taking her out to sea.

'That's why I've arranged for a stylist to drop by with some suitable outfits. All you have to do is pick one and be ready to leave at eleven,' he added, picking up his phone and punching in a number, his focus already on something else.

It was not a request but a demand, she thought as she walked slowly back to her room. Like every other word that came out of his mouth.

Part of her couldn't help but admire the absolute conviction with which he lived every moment of his life. He simply didn't acknowledge the possibility of refusal or rejection. But then why would he? From birth he had been surrounded by immutable certainties. His family's wealth. His parents' love. They, and his father in particular, had given him the confidence to expect, to demand what he wanted.

Chest tightening, she thought back to her own childhood, to how every single thing, every day, had seemed like a battle. Nothing had ever been easy or permanent. Always there had been that sense of sand shifting beneath her feet. The fear that if she closed her eyes when she opened them again everything would be gone.

Like when she'd come home from school that time and the sofa and television had disappeared—taken by Bill to clear a debt or cover a bet.

The sofa's feet had left four neat circular indentations in the carpet, like miniature crop circles. No matter how often she had vacuumed over them they hadn't faded.

Maybe they never would. Maybe they would stay there for ever. Like the scars inside her.

The scars that had kept her hiding in the shadows—scars that made it hard to trust other people, to trust herself.

Except when she made perfume. Then she was confident in her judgement.

She sighed. It was too late to worry about scars and trust. Now there was this.

There was Achileas.

And there was a 'them'…an 'us'. Only, unlike other couples, their relationship required a burden of proof. They needed to be seen. And so, for the first time in her life she would have to step out from the shadows and into the sunlight.

Two hours later, Effie tottered out onto the terrace, feeling like an underprepared understudy walking onstage.

It wasn't Virginie the stylist's fault. The dress was indisputably lovely. It was also nothing like any dress she'd ever worn before or would ever have chosen to wear. Skin-coloured, with short sleeves, and a pleated hemline that hovered above her knees. Virginie had paired it with wedge-heeled sandals.

She looked—she *felt*—naked.

She felt like someone had burrowed beneath her skin and taken over her body.

Achileas, who had been scrolling down the messages on his phone, turned. There was a moment of silence as the ripple of his gaze moved through her, and even though she tried to stop it her stomach knotted fiercely.

If their relationship had been real, he would have told her she looked beautiful and kissed her, but he just nodded and said, 'Good, you're here.'

Stretched taut between fantasy and reality, she could only manage a nod in reply. He had changed, too, into a linen suit. On some men, linen could look cheap and crumpled. But Achileas was not like most men. It didn't matter what he wore. Nothing could disguise the authority that was as much a part of him as those dazzling sapphire-blue eyes.

'Good,' he said again, and then he frowned. 'I almost forgot...' Reaching into his jacket, he pulled out a small square box. 'You'll need to put this on.'

A muscle was working in his jaw, as if he wanted to say something more, but instead he opened the box. She stared down at the engagement ring, her heart thumping so loudly she was surprised the villa's staff didn't come out to investigate the noise.

Feeling all thumbs beneath his scrutiny, she slid it clumsily onto her finger. Surely the ring wouldn't fit.

Astonishingly, it did, and she felt a sudden wild desire to laugh. Because it didn't feel real. It was as if she was dressing up in someone else's clothes like she had when she was a child. Only then it had been her mum's nightie—not a designer dress and a diamond that was probably worth more than her entire block of flats.

'Ready?'

He stared down at her, the slow burn of his gaze making her skin tingle. *No*, she thought.

'Yes,' she said quietly.

Picking up his napkin, Achileas glanced across the table to where Effie sat gazing down at the menu.

After arriving at Mykonos, they had wandered around the upmarket waterfront boutiques hand in hand, and now they were here having lunch at I Karydiá, a restaurant that was currently creating a big buzz among foodies in that part of the world.

Everything was going according to plan—*his*

plan. So, by rights he should be feeling good. Only for some reason nothing felt as it should.

But perhaps he shouldn't be surprised.

The day had started badly. He had woken early, in darkness, his body twitching like a sleeping dog chasing rabbits. But it was Effie who had been running in his dreams. Effie just out of reach, the pale soles of her delicate feet always one step ahead, as she darted through a landscape that was both familiar and alien. And he'd wanted to catch her, just as he had wanted to keep kissing her last night. More than kiss her, he had wanted to strip her, to stretch her out beneath him and open her body to his—

He gritted his teeth as his groin hardened painfully.

He had stopped himself—stopped both of them going further…going all the way. He'd had to. Sleeping with Effie would complicate an already fraught situation. But taking her virginity—

He felt a beat of frustration skim over his skin.

Dreaming about Effie had been unsettling enough, and lying there alone in bed, with lust tugging at his night-heightened senses, had been like an exquisite form of torture. In the end, he'd given up and got up. Without even bothering to get dressed, he had gone down to the lagoon, stripped off his pyjama shorts and swum until his muscles burned.

But the pain had been worth it.

Emerging from the water, he had felt everything suddenly become clear to him. He had been trying too hard, thinking he needed to treat her differently because she was going to be his wife. But in public, where it mattered, Effie was no different from any other woman.

There and then, he'd made up his mind to start over. Act as he always did. And if that meant hopscotching around the neighbouring islands on a boat or idling over a meal in the best restaurant in town then so be it.

This day out together was supposed to have pressed the reset button—only thanks to Effie he felt tenser than he had at the villa.

He scowled at a passing waiter. He'd seen how she lived. She should be excited by all this. Grateful, even. Okay, on the surface she was making all the right noises, looking up at him with those huge saucer eyes, but he knew she was faking it and that annoyed him.

Women didn't fake it with him.

Only it didn't make any sense for him to feel that way, because everything about the two of them *was* fake, and that annoyed him even more.

His eyes dropped to the graceful line of her throat, then lower, to a beauty spot the size of a pinhead at the top of her cleavage.

It didn't help seeing her dressed like that.

He'd thought it would. He'd assumed that if

she dressed like his previous girlfriends then it would be business as usual. He would feel attached rather than interdependent. But maybe because he was fighting to keep from touching her, he felt as if Effie was surrounded by some invisible glass barrier.

He thought back to the moment when she had walked out onto the terrace. With her huge brown eyes and those spindly legs, she had looked like a doe, picking her way through a forest. It was the first time she had worn something that didn't hang off her body, and *his* body had reacted viscerally—was still reacting—to the flare of her breasts and the sudden magician's reveal of all that flawlessly smooth bare skin.

'Are you ready to order, sir?'

The waiter had materialised by his elbow, but Effie chose that moment to shift in her seat, and as her legs brushed against his he momentarily lost the power of speech. Heart pounding, he braced his hand against the table, trying to clear his head.

'Yes,' he snapped, without looking at the waiter. 'We'll have the scallops and then the lamb. And a bottle of the Malagouzia.'

Her eyes darted to his face. She had, he knew, expected to choose her own food, but he'd done her yet another favour. It wasn't as if Michelin-starred restaurants were her stomping ground.

Their starters arrived promptly, followed by

the main course, both of which were delicious. Only he was too on edge to really enjoy either.

'Was everything to your satisfaction?' the waiter said as he took their plates.

'It was delicious, thank you.'

Effie looked up at the waiter and, watching her smile, Achileas felt the muscles in his arms bunch tightly. Her smile was gentle and miraculous…pure. It was like catching sight of a harvest moon.

The waiter clearly agreed with him, he thought irritably, his jaw hardening. It made him feel territorial in a way that seemed both shocking and justified.

He reached over and caught her hand. She blinked, and his gaze sharpened. She'd done something different to her hair. The sides were pulled back but the rest was loose. She had caught the sun a little too. It suited her…brought out the colour of her eyes. Less iced tea, more single malt whisky, he thought with a jolt, wondering how he had ever thought they were boring.

'I think we'll skip dessert, *agápi mou.*'

'And do what?'

As he opened his mouth to reply, the memory of how she'd kissed him yesterday rushed into his head like an unruly wave and his fingers tightened around hers. Sunlight was bouncing off the sea outside into the restaurant, making the waves appear to ripple over the walls, and now he felt almost as if they were underwater. Around them, the other diners seemed blurred and indistinct.

'Whatever you want.'

Her pupils flared and suddenly he forgot his frustration. He forgot to be angry with his father. He even forgot that they were pretending to be a couple. Suddenly all that mattered was that molten light in her eyes.

Everything was soft and simple and—

There was a clatter of cutlery and then a crash, and Effie's eyes jerked sideways.

He frowned.

'*Syngnómi*, sir.' Glancing over with an agonised expression on his face, the waiter ducked down to pick up the plates he'd dropped.

Achileas stared at him irritably, and then his irritation increased tenfold as Effie pulled her hand free and bent down to help pick up the knives and forks.

'Leave it,' he snapped, catching her arm. 'It's his job. Although maybe it shouldn't be.'

She stared at him, a flood of colour spilling across her cheeks. 'It was an accident,' she said.

'It's incompetence,' he retorted, irritated on all kinds of levels by her defensive remark. 'And if I was paying his wages he'd be fired. I don't pay people to be incompetent.'

Her chin jerked up. 'No, just compliant. Excuse me.'

Astonishingly, that last exchange and the accompanying small smile had been addressed not to him but the waiter, and before he even had a chance to react Effie had pushed back her chair. He watched incredulously as she wove swiftly through the restaurant. Judging by the sudden stillness in the room, he wasn't the only one struggling with incredulity at this development and, fuming, he tossed some notes onto the table and strode between the rigid diners to the door.

Outside in the street the sun was hot and bright—but not nearly as hot and bright as his temper. Grabbing her hand, he pulled her down a deserted side-street. 'Don't ever speak to me like that again.'

She turned towards him, her eyes flashing almost gold in the light. 'That won't be a problem,' she said quietly.

'Good.'

'Because I don't plan on speaking to you again.' She stepped past him.

What? He spun round, staring after her. Stunned. Speechless. Cut off at the knees. What was she talking about? His jaw clenched. And where was she going?

He caught up with her by the quay. And that was a first. Never in his life had he chased after a woman. 'What the hell do you think you're doing?'

'I'm going back to the villa.'

'I'm not ready to go back yet.'

Her eyes flashed fire again, and despite his fury there was something glorious in her anger. 'It suits me fine to go alone.'

It was just like in London. Behind him, he could sense his bodyguards, studiously staring anywhere but at their boss. He swore under his breath. Only this time—incredibly—she really was leaving. With or without him.

The trip back to the villa was conducted in total silence. Back at the island, she stepped off the boat as it nudged up against the jetty, and once again he found himself in the extraordinary position of having to chase after her.

He stalked through the villa, blood pounding through his veins. 'What is wrong with you?' he demanded.

They were standing in her bedroom. She had kicked off her shoes and with her bare feet and flushed cheeks she looked young and defiant, like some student revolutionary.

'Me? Oh, I'm naive and stupid. But you already know that.'

'No, what you are is ungrateful,' he snarled. 'I take you out to lunch. I buy you a dress. I give you a ring. Do you know how many women would change places with you?'

'Yes.' Her eyes flared. '*None*. That's why I'm here. And you didn't buy *me* a dress or a ring. You bought those for your imaginary wife-to-be.'

'Not imaginary. We have a deal.' He bit out the words.

'And there was nothing in that deal that said I have to stand by and watch you treat people like dirt.'

He stared at her in shock, more shocked than if she had hurled her shoes at his head. And for a short, tense pause it almost felt like she had.

'That's what this is about?' His eyes narrowed. 'He's a *waiter*.'

The look of disgust on her face was not one he'd ever experienced or was likely to forget. 'He's a person. With a name. He's not just "the kitchen" or "Housekeeping". And I'm a person too, Achileas.'

He stared at her, jolted. It was the first time she had called him by his name. 'I know that.'

'Do you?' Her mouth trembled. 'If that's true then I don't know why you made me get all dressed up.'

'You had nothing to wear. Nothing appropriate, that is.' He made no attempt to soften his tone.

She shook her head, her eyes huge and bright—too bright. 'You're wrong. I do have something to wear. I wear it every day at work. I have a dress and an apron.'

The tightness was back in his chest.

'You're not making any sense, Effie.'

'Then let me explain. You talked to me in that restaurant like I was a maid. So why didn't you just let me dress like one?'

'That's not what happened—'

'It's exactly what happened. When I'm in my uniform I can deal with people like you, being rude and dismissive and treating me like I'm nothing. But you—you took that away from me.'

Something in her voice pressed against the ache in his chest. 'Effie—'

He reached out but she took a step backwards, holding up her hand as if that could stop him.

Except it did.

'I know I'm not beautiful or clever or rich. I know I don't matter very much in the scheme of things. But nobody's ever made me feel that worthless.'

He stared at her in silence, feeling emotions he hardly recognised. 'That's not what… I didn't mean for that to happen… What are you doing?'

She had turned away and was picking up things: a book, some pyjamas.

'I'm going to pack.'

'No.' He crossed the room in two strides. 'You can't do that.'

'Oh, yes, I can.'

Her mouth was trembling, but he could see in her eyes that she was serious.

'I mean, what are you going to do? Fire me? Give me a bad reference? I know you haven't quite got your head around this, Achileas, but I'm not your employee.'

'I know that,' he said again. 'But we have a deal.'

Her eyes found his, and if her anger had shocked him her pain felt like an actual blow.

'You know what? I've been poor all my life, but some things are more important than money.'

He blocked her path. 'Please, don't go. I don't want you to go.'

'And this is all about what you want—'

'That's not what I meant. You're putting words into my mouth.'

She stared up at him. 'In that case your next line is, *I'll leave you to pack.*'

He frowned. 'Effie, please... I don't know how to—' There was a note he didn't recognise in his voice. 'Look, I'm sorry. I'm sorry for what I said, and for hurting you.'

'You probably always are.'

Her voice had changed too. The anger had faded, and in its place was a bruise that made him forget his own feelings.

'But this isn't just about you. It's about me.' She shook her head. 'And I can't do this. I thought I could, but I can't lie to myself as well as everyone else. I'll wear any dress, I'll put my hair up or down, but I can't, and I won't behave in a way that I know is wrong and pretend that it's okay. I promised myself I would never do that…that I would never be like him—'

He didn't understand what she was talking about, but he understood the pain in her eyes.

'Be like who?' With shock, he realised that he wanted to know. He wanted to know who had hurt her.

And then he wanted to hurt them.

'It doesn't matter.' She wrapped her arms around her stomach as if it ached.

'It does to me. I know you probably don't believe me, and I understand why you would feel like that, but if you could just give me a chance.' He took a breath. 'Please, Effie…'

Silence.

He made himself wait, although he couldn't remember ever doing so before—for anyone. To wait was to be powerless. But he would wait an eternity if that was what it took to make that terrible rigidity melt from her body.

The silence lengthened, and then, in a voice so low he could hardly hear it, she said, 'My father Bill.'

Her father.

He felt his chest tighten. He had been so wrapped up in battling his own paternal demons he had never imagined she would have any of her own.

'Why don't you want to be like him?'

'He's a gambler.' Her mouth twisted as if she might smile, but she didn't smile. 'It sounds reckless and exciting, doesn't it? Like being a highwayman or a pirate. But it's not like that when you're living with one. It's terrifying. Every morning you wake up knowing that anything can happen. One day he spent a month's wages in a couple of minutes.'

'What did he gamble on?'

She stared past him, her elbows locked tight against her body. 'In the beginning it was horses, but then it was online roulette. He won occasionally. But mostly he lost. Because that's how it works. And he lied. All the time. To my mum. To me. To himself.'

The knuckles of her hands were white now.

'Are they still together?' he asked.

She shook her head. 'He left when I was fourteen. He used to come back sometimes. Let himself in and take whatever he could find. Pawn it or sell it...'

Her voice faded, but he didn't need to hear more to hear the deeper truth: that her father had robbed her of more than just possessions. He'd taken her trust.

Anger raged inside him—an anger that was separate from and yet mixed in with his own. Anger at the bad fathers of the world and the lies they told...the lies they forced others to tell. And with himself too, for making her lie. For pressing against the bruise.

'Every time he made the same promise. "This is the last time." But it never was. He can't help himself. He doesn't want to help himself. And he won't let anyone else help him either.'

He stared down at her, stricken, understanding that sense of powerlessness, and then without any kind of conscious intent to do so, he reached out and took her hands. 'You were a child.'

She shook her head again. 'I didn't do enough. Look at what you're doing for *your* father.'

His chest tightened as she looked up at him, her face quivering.

'I should have tried harder...' she said. 'Tried to make him listen—'

It was on the tip of his tongue to tell her the truth. To tell her that he wasn't who she thought he was. That he was lying to Andreas not out of love but in revenge. To get back at the father who had disowned him. The father he had met only twice in his life.

Only he couldn't do it.

He felt his cowardice in the pit of his stomach as his hands tightened around hers.

'I doubt he would have listened,' he said, gentling his voice so that she wouldn't hear his bitterness and pain. 'He didn't listen to anything your mother had to say.'

There was a small silence. 'She didn't say anything.' Her shoulders flexed beneath a weight he hadn't known she was carrying. 'She couldn't. She had a stroke when I was thirteen and it affected her speech.'

Shock blotted out his own painful memories. But if her father had left when she was fourteen—

'Who took care of her?'

But even before she spoke, he knew the answer.

'I did,' she whispered. 'We had some help, but then I left school when I was sixteen and we managed just fine.' Her eyes were shining now, with unshed tears not of pity but of pride. 'Only then she had another stroke, a year ago, and now she's in a home because she needs specialist care. And I need her to be safe.'

And that was why she was here. With him.

The muscles of his face contracted. 'She'll always be safe. Because she's got you.'

He tried to smile, but the brightness in her eyes made it suddenly impossible to do anything but pull her against him as the tears she had been holding back started to fall.

She was so young—too young to have gone through all of that—and he hated it that it had happened. Once again, he found himself hating all bad fathers. Hating himself most of all.

His arms tightened around her. 'And you've got me.'

'But that's the point. I don't have you.' She tilted her tear-stained face up to meet his. 'You want this to work. You want us to look like a couple, but that's not going to be enough. We have to *be* a couple. Maybe not a "for ever" couple, who love each other and want to spend their lives together, but this has to be more than just playing dress-up.'

'I get that—'

But she was shaking her head.

'No, you don't. You think you can just give me clothes and a ring and that's your part done. Then it's on me to convince people. All you have to do is get the bill. And you can't forget even for a moment that you're paying, because deep down you think having money makes you a better person. But if you can't forget it, if you don't see me as your equal, then everyone—including your father—is going to know we're faking it.'

Achileas stared down at her dazedly. At work he was used to bragging hyperbole and brash rhetoric. Outside of work the people he mixed with had a swaggering language that mirrored their splashy lifestyle. And yet somehow Effie's quiet manner reinforced rather than reduced the truth of her words.

She really was one of a kind.

'You're not my equal, Effie,' he said slowly. 'You're way smarter than me.' Pulling her closer, he stroked her hair gently. 'I'm sorry. I'm an idiot. I thought this would be easy. I thought I could just slot you into my life. That's why I took you to lunch. Why I made you get dressed up.'

He hesitated, not wanting to admit to that rush of jealousy, but then he thought about her honesty and all the truths he was holding back. Surely, he could admit this.

'Only then you came onto the terrace in that dress, and I didn't like it.'

Effie frowned. 'I thought you wanted me to get dressed up.'

'I did. But only for me.'

Her eyes fluttered to his face, but she didn't react.

'And I didn't like it when you smiled at the waiter. I wanted you to smile at me. I wanted you to like me.'

There was another silence, and her voice was scratchy when she answered. 'I do like you. You know I like you. But you said—'

'I know what I said.'

He had wanted it to be true. Wanted to be free of that fierce, unforeseen hunger that made no sense. Only having pushed Effie away, he had been left with an emptiness that had filled his lungs, crowding out the air so it had felt as if he was drowning. And he had panicked. It was no excuse, but that was why he'd behaved as he had.

'I was lying. To you. To myself.' He swallowed, hard. 'The truth is, I do care. And you were right about the money. My job, my life makes things binary. You're either a have or a have-not. But a wise woman once told me there was more to life than money and she was right. I can't do this on my own. I need you, Effie. And I want you. I want you so badly that I can't think about anything else.'

He could see the faint tremor beneath her skin, the flush across her cheeks. 'But if you've changed your mind...'

There was a long, pulsing silence, and then she let out a long, slow breath, as if she was letting go of more than just air. She shook her head. 'I haven't,' she said quietly.

CHAPTER SEVEN

STARING DOWN AT EFFIE, Achileas felt the blood roaring in his ears. There was still time to stop this, to turn away. But he didn't want to turn away or stop. He couldn't.

And the truth of that swelled up, washing over him as he leaned forward and kissed her gently, his hands caressing, his fingers sliding over the smooth bones of her ribs, down to her hips, tilting her pelvis towards him, feeling the heat of her skin through the fabric of her dress.

He moved his lips across hers, tracing their shape, taking his time, more time than he ever normally would, and not just because she was a virgin. He wanted to taste her…to lick the heat from her mouth into his. And she tasted so good. Sweet like sun-warmed honey and more intoxicating than wine.

Her lower lip quivered, and he felt her breathe out shakily and he kissed her more deeply, kissed her until she was shivering against him, her skin, her limbs, her body trembling uncontrollably.

Everything about her was soft and pliant, and the need to touch more of her was pounding through his body. He wanted her. Only it was more than just wanting. His body ached with a hunger he had never felt before.

Hs hands rose up to cup her breasts, his groin hardening as her nipples stiffened against the palms of his hands.

She moaned softly, her fingers digging into the flesh of his arms. 'Should I take off my dress now?'

Her question, delivered in that quiet, precise way of hers, almost sent him over the edge. His face burning with shock and desire, he drew her against him, trying to slow his pulse, to calm the tangle of heat and hunger churning deep inside him.

'Would you like to?'

Effie stared up at Achileas, her heart pounding. 'Yes…' she whispered, although she wasn't sure that it would be enough.

She felt as if she'd spent too long in the sun— as if the heat had burrowed through her clothes into her body…if only she could unzip her skin.

Her pulse twitched as he kissed her neck, the bristles of his stubble sending a flood of hot sensation through her limbs and she shivered inside, drinking in the smell of him—part skin, part sunlight, all male.

'I'd like it too,' he said hoarsely.

His fingers moved to the front of her dress, and she felt the fabric tug as he pulled the buttons through the tiny holes. He was breathing unsteadily. As the last button popped free, he slid his hand slowly along her collarbone. Slipping the dress off her shoulders, he let it fall to her feet.

The air felt cool against her skin. She was wearing simple white underwear. Cotton, not silk. No lace. Reaching behind her back, she unhooked her bra, letting it drop beside her dress. Now she was naked except for her panties. She hooked her fingers into the fabric—

'Stop.'

His voice scraped across her skin, and she stared up at him dazedly.

'Let down your hair.'

The words, so stark, so direct, sent flickers of feeling everywhere. Hands trembling, she slid her fingers through her hair, jerking it free of the band at the nape of her neck.

'Now shake your head,' he ordered.

Dry-mouthed, she did as he commanded, staring up at him, her throat swollen with something that didn't have a name as her hair tumbled to her shoulders. No one had ever made her feel like this...so hungry and so helpless at the same time.

His gaze was dark and steady and unblinking. She could feel the intensity of his concentration, see the pulse beating in his neck, beating out the same rhythm as her heart, as if they were flamenco dancers stamping out a *zapateado*.

He muttered something in Greek, and then he reached out and caressed her cheek. The heat of his fingers blossomed deep inside her and her skin ached for his touch. Every cell, every single centimetre of skin, was humming.

She wanted to touch him too. Wanted to lean in closer, to explore him.

Even as she thought it, she moved her hand to the buttons on his shirt. With fingers that shook slightly, she pushed the shirt off his shoulders. The cuffs caught at his wrists, and he swore softly, jerking his hands free before drawing her closer.

Staring down at his bare chest, she swallowed. She was nervous, but mostly she was turned on. Her fingers touched the waistband of his trousers and the muscles of his stomach twitched, as if touched by some invisible current. And then he was leaning forward, kissing her hungrily, parting her lips, sliding his hand up her back to the nape of her neck.

The ridge of his erection was pushing into her stomach. Without breaking the kiss, he lifted her slightly so that it pressed against her pelvic bone, and a sharp heat she had never felt before flared between her thighs.

Head spinning, melting on the inside, she

moaned, shuddering as his fingers brushed lightly over her taut nipples. His tongue was in her mouth, making her stomach clench and ache. It made her think of his hard body on hers. Inside her.

She reached for the zip of his trousers. Grunting, he jerked backwards, his hands catching her wrists. He was breathing deeply, and there was a dark flush along his cheekbones. For a moment he stared down at her intently, so intently that her skin tingled wherever his gaze touched.

'Let's go to bed,' he said softly, and he pulled her backwards, leading her by the wrists.

She let him. It was what she wanted. It was all she wanted. He was all she wanted. And he wanted her. Here and now. Everything else might be a lie, but this was their truth.

She watched dizzily as he stripped off first his trousers and then his boxer shorts.

Now he was as naked as he had been that morning.

Only this time he was bigger, harder...

Suddenly she could hardly breathe. Tiny waves of panic were rippling through her, colliding with the frantic beat of her heart.

'Don't be scared,' he said.

'I'm not.' She hesitated. 'Well, maybe I am a little bit.'

'You don't need to be. I won't hurt you. I won't let anyone hurt you.' His eyes were suddenly dark blue and fierce, his face granite-hard like his warrior namesake's.

He dipped his head and kissed her gently, his hands firm, compelling, sliding slowly over her body, pulling her onto the bed beneath him.

She drew in a sharp breath as his lips found the hollow beneath her ear, and then she dragged in another as his lips trailed down her neck slowly, to her collarbone, and then lower still to her breast.

As his mouth closed around her nipple, her fingers bit into the thick muscles of his arm. She felt him tense.

'Is that okay?' he asked.

'Yes,' she whispered. *'Yes...'* she said again.

It was more than okay—only she didn't have the words or thoughts. Everything was dissolving except this fierce, insatiable hunger. Helplessly, she arched against him, pressing closer, wanting more, needing to satisfy the ache inside her.

Whimpering, she grabbed his hand, flattening the palm against the staccato pulse beating between her legs.

'Effie...' He groaned her name and she felt him shift against her.

'I want you,' she said.

He stared down at her, his eyes dark with passion. 'You have me,' he said hoarsely.

'No. Inside me.'

His dense black lashes fluttered at her words and her heart pounded. It might hurt, but she wanted to feel him. To feel his heat and strength.

Her hand flexed against him as he started to stroke her through the damp cotton. The tip of his finger slipped beneath the fabric and her hand balled into a fist as he brushed against her clitoris. She arched upwards, legs shaking. Heat was swamping her.

'Is that okay?' he said again.

Nodding, she clasped his face, pressing a desperate kiss to his mouth, her breath catching as his fingers caressed her. She felt him move, his body pushing forward, and her own body tensed in sudden panic. How could this work? He would be too big...

'Don't be scared,' he whispered again. His lips brushed against her mouth, her shoulder, her collarbone. 'It if hurts, or if you change your mind, we can stop any time—'

'I don't want to stop.'

He leaned over her, kissed her, and then his hands slid slowly under her bottom, and he pulled her panties down over her thighs, lifting her further up the bed, stretching out over her, parting her legs.

'I'll just get a condom.'

She watched as he reached onto the floor for his trousers, shivering with nerves and anticipation as he rolled on the condom.

Breathing out unsteadily, he rubbed the tip of his erection between her thighs, pushing into the slick heat a little deeper each time, and she responded instinctively, opening her body to his, moving her hands to his hips.

'That's it...' he murmured. 'Like that.'

His face was taut with concentration, his eyes burning into hers, and then he lifted her hips and slid into her.

Her breath caught. He felt hot and sleek and big, too big and for a moment she concentrated on absorbing the size of him. Then it stung a little, stretched a little more and her hands braced against his chest.

Instantly, he stilled. 'It's okay,' he said softly. 'Take all the time you need. Your body is just getting used to how it feels.'

She nodded. He was right, she thought a moment later as the muscles in her thighs loosened.

He shifted, taking more of his weight on his elbows, and looked down at her as if he was trying to commit her face to memory. 'Now move with me.'

Her pulse quickened as his mouth found hers, his kiss taking her with him so that soon her head was spinning, and her muscles were relaxed. Her hips lifted to accept him, her body stretching, opening, the pulse between her thighs getting faster and more insistent.

She reached for him blindly, wrapping her

arms around his shoulders, chasing the pulse as he drove into her. Her skin felt white-hot. Her blood was like lava. She was melting inside, dissolving with need, and now her muscles were tightening again, tightening around him, trying to hold on to him, gripping tighter and tighter—

Her mouth opened and she made a sort of keening, one-syllable noise that swelled inside her unbidden. And then her body tensed, and she arched, a barb of sharp pleasure jerking her hips against his, flames rippling through her as she shuddered helplessly beneath him.

She felt Achileas thrust deeper. He buried his hands in her hair and his mouth covered hers as he reared forward, taking her with him, his body surging inside hers.

He grunted, limbs twitching, and she felt him ease down against her, his skin hot and damp.

Heart pounding, Effie stared dazedly across the room, half expecting to see the beautiful dressing table on fire. Or on its side, drawers emptied. Or the curtains ripped from the windows. Anything that would reflect the immensity of what had just happened inside the room.

But it was all exactly the same.

For a moment she listened to the sound of their fractured breathing, resting her fingers limply against his shoulders. Her lips were soft and puffy from all their kissing, and she felt like a piece of clay that Achileas had shaped with his hands into something new and beautiful.

Was that how she was supposed to feel? Was that what everyone's first time was like? So powerful and sensual? She hoped it was.

It had been just so beautiful…so utterly beyond anything she could have imagined. She'd had no idea that hands could stir and torment to such a pitch of pleasure. Or that skin could be so sensitive. Even now everything felt magnified and sensual—the shudder of his breath against her shoulder, the weight of his hand in her hair.

Achileas's breath.

Achileas's hand.

She felt her chest tighten. Everything about him was so perfect, and it had felt so good, so right, when he'd moved against her, inside her…

He was still inside her now, and nobody ever told you about that part. How good, how right, how perfect it felt. To lie there as one, bodies fused.

Her heart squeezed. He had made her want so much and now it was over.

'I didn't hurt you, did I?'

Achileas was looking down at her intently.

'No.' She shook her head, wanting to tell him the truth.

But how could she? He had told her that she could change her mind and that he would stop. But she hadn't wanted him to stop, and it had changed everything. He had changed everything. Changed her from the inside out. Changed her understanding of the world and herself. He had made her want things, and she had asked and taken what she wanted in ways she had never done before.

His eyes held hers for a moment and then he shifted backwards, lifting his body carefully off hers.

Still floating on clouds, she reached for him.

'No, you stay here,' he said, and she felt a sharp pang like an actual physical loss as he rolled off the bed and disappeared into the bathroom.

But what had she expected him to do? He was hardly going to keep holding her against him afterwards, like a lover. And although they hadn't discussed it, it was obvious now that there was a reason for that.

Her first time with Achileas would also be her only time with him. The logical part of her brain had accepted that. But the other part—the part that had surrendered to him completely—couldn't seem to let go.

Her breath was trapped in her throat as she watched him walk back into the bedroom, carelessly, casually naked, and a riot of sensations and emotions stormed through her body. His eyes were unreadable, his face set into an expression she couldn't even begin to fathom. And then her heart skipped a beat as he climbed back into bed, and she realised that he had just been getting rid of the condom.

Gazing down at his muscular body, she felt her skin grow warm. She was not quite embarrassed, but a little shy at her naivety. And at his nudity. He was just so big and masculine and naked.

And still aroused.

She felt her body ripple back to life.

'What are you thinking about?' Achileas asked.

He was looking down at her, his blue eyes intent on her face. She tried to smile, to distance herself from the ache in her breasts and the flare of heat between her thighs.

'I was just thinking that now I understand what all the fuss is about.' They were lying close together. Close enough that she could feel the furnace heat of his skin, and better still breathe in his delicious maleness. 'I didn't before.'

He tipped his head back, his mouth curling into a question mark. 'Fuss about what?'

'Sex.' She bit her lip. 'I didn't get what people meant. But now I can see why they say it makes the world go round.'

The corners of his mouth tugged upwards. 'I think you'll find that's money.'

She pulled in a breath, lost in his smile. He was right, it was money, but her brain didn't seem to be working properly.

Fighting to keep her voice casual, she said, 'So what do they say about sex?'

He reached out and brushed her hair away from her breast, letting his hand graze against the nipple until it hardened.

'I don't know and I don't care what they say. I only care about what you say. What you want.' His teasing smile faded and slowly he trailed his fingertips from her aching breast down over the curve of her hip to the triangle of hair between her thighs. 'What you like.'

She stared up at him in silence. That was easy: she liked him.

A lot.

Too much.

But this was just how people talked about sex, wasn't it?

He wasn't being serious.

Was he?

Suddenly she wished she knew more…had experienced more. Like Tamara and all those other women from his world. She knew so little about how sex worked, so little about this kind of intimate moment.

Her shoulders shifted. But she did know that there had already been too many lies in her life, too many hidden truths. She knew, too, that she wanted his hand to keep sliding over her skin.

So why not take a risk tinier than the last?

She cleared her throat. 'I like it when you touch me.'

His eyes on hers were dark and unreadable and she felt a wildness inside her, both hope and panic, as the silence stretched between them. And then he moved closer and kissed her softly… so softly that his lips barely whispered against hers. And yet she could feel the heat beneath, and the power. Always the power.

'I like it too.' His voice was rough sounding, as if it was an effort to admit it even to himself, and then his hands moved to her back, and he drew her closer. 'And I'd like to keep touching you, and for you to keep touching me.'

She stared at him mutely, shaking his words like a gold prospector, turning them over, sifting them, sieving them inside her head.

A short time ago she had been living on her own, living half a life in her tiny London flat. Now she was on an island, a private island in the middle of the Aegean, sharing a bed with a man. And not just a bed; she knew what Achileas's hard body felt like inside hers and the speed of change made her feel dizzy.

Her eyes skimmed back and forth over the smooth, contours of his chest and stomach, dipping lower with each pass. Years of living with the unknown had made her fear uncertainty, and she knew that to keep touching him would have unknowable consequences.

But right now, here in this moment, not touching him again was unthinkable.

She met his gaze, her pulse quivering. 'Do you mean like this?' Reaching up, she touched his face lightly.

'Yes, like that.'

He didn't move a muscle, but something flickered in his eyes like a flame, and she felt an answering flutter of heat low in her stomach. Impossible to ignore.

Now she touched his chest. His skin was warm and damp, and she could feel his heart beating through her fingertips. 'And like this?'

He nodded.

She hesitated, and then her hand moved from his chest to his groin. She felt his sudden stillness, heard his sharp intake of breath like the backdraught in a burning building. 'And what about this? Do you like that?'

He didn't answer. Instead, he leaned into her, lifting her face to his, and kissed her—kissed her until she couldn't speak or think or breathe, opening her mouth to his, giving her his answer. Her belly clenched, tight and hot and aching, as he rolled her under his body, and everything she wanted in the world was there with him.

CHAPTER EIGHT

NAKED, ACHILEAS STEPPED onto the balcony. He hesitated a moment, glancing back at the bed where Effie was sleeping. She had fallen asleep in his arms, her soft body curled around his, and he wanted to sleep too. But everything kept replaying in his head.

Starting with what had just happened.

His heart was suddenly speeding.

Even now it blew his mind, and a part of him couldn't quite accept what they had done. But the facts were clear and irrefutable. Effie had been a virgin when they'd walked back into the villa this afternoon and now, she wasn't.

Now she was his.

He glanced back to the woman on the bed again.

Her hair was spilling over the pillow like warm buckwheat honey. Thinking about how he'd tangled his hands through it as she clung to him, and the noises she had made, turned his breathing inside out, so that he felt almost faint.

She had been sweet and pliable, like spun sugar, and her body had been a revelation. Small, firm breasts, a waist he could fit his hands around, and that throat...

Her first time: not his.

Although in some ways it had felt as if it was. There had been a newness and a nervousness in him he had never felt before, even when he'd lost his own virginity. The desire to give pleasure, to take care of her was not unique—for him, good sex was always about mutual satisfaction. But Effie had been his first time with a virgin, and he had found it impossible to keep his usual distance.

Touching her, watching her face soften, feeling her body open to his, had made him feel—

What?

He didn't know. Other than anger, he shied away from emotions. More than one of his former girlfriends had accused him of lacking emotional intelligence. Maybe that was why he was finding it so hard to explain away these feelings now—feelings he couldn't even name, much less process.

But his confusion was probably down to it being completely unplanned. Truthfully, he thought he'd blown the whole damn thing back in the restaurant. He had been so tense, had behaved so unreasonably, and Effie—well, she had been furious.

And his fury had matched hers.

He felt his spine stiffen as he remembered his blind, ungovernable rage.

Nobody had ever talked to him as she had. From an early age, his temper, and his implacable determination to win at any cost had meant that everyone—including grown men twice her size—had backed down, placated him, or simply turned a blind eye to his worst behaviour.

Not Effie.

She had called him out. Told him the truth. She had held a mirror to his face; and he hadn't liked what he saw.

His chest felt tight against his ribs.

Confronting his failings had been hard, painful, *shocking*. But what had snuffed out his fury...the dark, impenetrable, all-consuming rage that clung to him like a shadow even on a cloudy day...was something else entirely. It was what Effie had told him about her father and her mother.

His fingers tightened around the rail.

When he was being rational, reasonable, he knew gambling was a sickness, and that therefore blame was inappropriate, but picturing Effie living in that situation made him want to rage at a higher authority.

Or punch something.

No wonder lying was such an anathema to her.

He stared out to sea, watching the waves break the surface, thinking back to their first meeting outside the Stanmore. Little Miss Nobody: that was what he'd called her then. And he'd been so sure of who she was. Small. Unimportant. A means to an end.

And, yes, she was small. But she was also talented and smart. Strong.

What she had done for her mother was nothing short of remarkable. Like him, she had turned her life around. His mouth thinned. The difference was, Effie had done it out of love—not anger and a desire for revenge.

He was glad. Grateful. So much of his life had been spent trying to push back the darkness he carried inside, and her strength, her purity of motive, was a tiny, flickering candle. It was making him question the man he had become. She was making him question the man he had become. The man he wanted to be after all this was over. On that basis Effie was way more than a means to an end.

And yet he was still lying to her.

He turned away from the restless sea.

Even after she had revealed so much of herself to him, he hadn't told her the truth about Andreas. He lacked her courage, and he hated that. But he couldn't tell her that his father had never wanted him. Or that even now Andreas's love and acceptance came with a condition.

How could he do that when she was the condition?

Later. He would tell her later, when everything between them was more settled, and after that they would face his father together. Then, when it was all over, she would leave, and he would get on with his life. A life without his dark burden.

His eyes narrowed. In the bedroom Effie was awake, and right now there was a new item at the top of his agenda. In fact, there was only one item, *one agenda*...and he walked towards her.

'What are you doing out here? Apart from wearing too much clothing.'

Effie jumped. A pair of warm hands slid around her waist and Achileas's stubbled jaw grazed her throat as he kissed her softly.

'I was just watching the boats. There's so many of them today.'

His fingers tiptoed beneath her shirt—*his* shirt, technically—and instantly she could feel herself sliding into that yielding place between the warmth of his hands and the sudden pounding of her heart.

'It's that time of year,' he murmured. 'It's the Galanólefki Ball this weekend.'

'What's that?'

He moved closer, and she felt more of that same mix of weakness and wonder as his body fitted around hers, hard where she was soft.

'It's an annual fundraising ball in aid of a

selection of children's charities, hosted at the Hipparchus Observatory in Athens. A glitzy gala night attended by local luminaries and global celebrities. Or that's what it says in the papers.'

His mouth had found the sensitive hollow just below her ear and she felt her pulse leap beneath his lips. Resisting the urge to let him explore further, she turned in the circle of his arms.

'What is Gala…? Gala—?' She stumbled over the word, distracted by the miraculous contours of his bare chest.

'Gal-an-ó-lefki,' he said slowly. 'It's what the Greeks call their flag. Like you have the Union Jack. It means blue and white. That's the dress code. It's a big deal. Wall-to-wall billionaires, and it does a lot of good. The ticket price alone raises millions.'

His eyes tracked the flotilla of white yachts slicing through the blue waves and she sensed that he was debating something.

'Actually, Arete is one of the sponsors.'

'It is?'

They were talking easily. Like a couple, in fact. She was still coming to terms with that. With how much things had changed between them over the last few days. Three days, in fact. Three days since she had told Achileas the truth about her father's gambling and her mum's illness.

He had been angry. Of course. He was Achilleas. But he had put his anger aside and he had held her against him, his arms tight around her body, as if he wanted to keep her safe. Wanted her to know he would keep her safe.

And she wanted that too. But most of all she wanted him.

Her throat was suddenly so dry it hurt to swallow. It was three days since she had lost her virginity, and her knowledge of sex and bodies—both her own and his—had grown exponentially hour by hour. Three days in which the half-formed fantasies she'd had about sex had been swept away by a man who had initiated her into an A to Z of positions and techniques that she was pretty sure few people even knew existed.

Her stomach cartwheeled. Somehow, he made sex feel like the most natural thing in the world, and intensely, mind-meltingly erotic. She simply couldn't imagine a better first lover.

A better lover.

Her ribs were suddenly too tight. Not that they were *making love*. She might be new to all this, but she understood enough to know that even though it felt like a wildness in her blood this was just sex.

'You sound surprised.' He was staring at her intently, an eyebrow raised, the blue of his eyes rivalling the spring sky above their heads.

She shook her head. 'I'm not surprised. I know you can be a good person.'

In bed, he was gentle, teasing, sometimes fierce and demanding. But he was always patient and generous and focused on every beat of her blood.

'You do?' He raised an eyebrow, as if he was reading her mind—which, to be fair, he probably was.

'You were kind to me when I told you about my father,' she said, as evenly as she could.

'You were upset.' His voice was cool. 'I did what any normal person would do.'

She stared at him, confused. There was a tension around his mouth that hadn't been there before, but why? It was almost as if she had accused him of something bad.

'What about this…us?' she said quietly. 'There's not many sons who would do what you're doing for their father?'

'And you think that makes me a good person?'

Before she could reply he shifted against her, his mouth curling into something that was not quite a smile. 'I'm flattered I've gone up in your estimation. But as far as the ball goes our sponsorship is good for business. Good for the charities. It's a fun evening. Everyone's happy.'

Except he didn't sound happy. The tension had transferred to his voice. Was it something to do with the ball? Did his father expect him to attend? Was he not going because of her?

'It sounds amazing. A once-in-a-lifetime experience.'

His gaze sharpened on her face. 'Are you saying you want to go?'

Was she? Three days ago, the idea would have terrified her. But now it didn't seem so scary. There was a truth to their relationship now…even if it wasn't the whole truth and nothing but the truth. And she wanted to take that tension from Achileas's body.

'Maybe,' she said, trying to keep her voice light.

'Really? It's just that the other day you said we should wait a little. Get our story straight.'

'That was then. Things are different now. We know each other better.'

His pupils flared. 'Yes, we do,' he said softly, and the dark shimmer in his voice reached inside her and prised her open.

Trying to ignore the maddening heat storming through her body, she said, 'And it would be a good place to be seen together in public.'

He nodded, and then his eyes narrowed, fixing on something past her shoulder. She shifted in his arms. Out at sea, yet another ship had appeared. It was moving slowly, like some oversized prehistoric monster, and beside it even the huge superyachts looked as tiny and insubstantial as dinghies.

'That is the biggest boat I've ever seen.'

'They can be bigger. That one, *The Tiphys*, is about the length of two football pitches—two hundred and sixty metres, to be precise.'

She blinked. 'How on earth do you know that?'

Was there some kind of marine equivalent of trainspotting? Although it didn't seem likely it would be Achileas's cup of tea.

Next to her, Achileas was silent. Then, 'See that logo on the bow? That's an Alexios ship. It's owned by Andreas Alexios.'

She had heard the name. Anyone not living under a rock had heard of the Alexios Shipping Group. Alexios was a name like Onassis or Niarchos. A name that conjured up images of proud, dark-eyed men standing on the decks of their shimmering oversized yachts, dictating the mood of the Aegean like modern-day Poseidons.

'Is he a friend of yours?'

He shook his head. 'Not a friend, no.' There was a short, taut pause, and then he added coolly, 'He's my father.'

His father. She stared at him in confusion. His father was *that* Andreas. Why, then, was he not Achileas Alexios?

Beside her, Achileas was still, but there was a kind of anticipatory tension vibrating in the air, like in that moment before the magician pulls a rabbit from a hat. Glancing up at his proud profile, she knew why he had not taken his father's name. Achileas was exactly the kind of man who would want to prove himself, want his success to be his own and not the result of any nepotistic bias.

'He must be very proud of you,' she said softly. 'For achieving so much without making use of his name.' Lifting her chin, she smiled a little shyly. 'Actually, I changed my name too.'

'You did?'

She felt his arms tighten around her, felt the first ripple of longing as he drew her closer. 'Well, maybe not changed. Just shortened. My real name is Josephine, but no one's ever called me that. Except the vicar when he christened me.'

'It's a beautiful name. You probably just needed time to grow into it.'

Her heart jumped as he reached out and tucked a strand of hair behind her ear.

'And now you have. So, do you want to come to the ball with me, Josephine?'

The heat in his voice as he said her name shuddered through her, kicking up sparks. 'Yes,' she said hoarsely.

'Then I'll go and make a few calls.' Reaching out, he took hold of her shirt, pinching the fab-

ric between his fingers to pull her against him.
'First, though, I'm going to need this back.'

He undid the top button, then the next one
down, his mouth finding hers as the shirt slid
from her shoulders, and then he was walking her
backwards into the bedroom towards the bed...

CHAPTER NINE

IT WAS ONE of the lesser-known benefits of being very wealthy, Achileas thought, settling back on the sofa, and stretching out his legs, that time became somewhat irrelevant. You could never be late or early, because essentially you *were* the board meeting or the dinner party or the charity lunch. When you arrived, everything started. And whenever you decided to leave there was always a car waiting at the kerb to take you where you wanted to go next.

But, rich or poor, some things didn't change. And that was why he was sitting here fully dressed, waiting for Effie. Or was it Josephine? He liked both names, but if he was being honest what he liked most was knowing that she was *his* Josephine. That nobody else had ever called her by that name.

If he was being honest.

The words rolled around inside his head like a bottle on a bar room floor. Only he wasn't being honest. Far from it.

And maybe at the beginning that had been the right, the only thing to do. He hadn't been about to share the details of his life with some random chambermaid. But there was nothing random about his relationship with Effie now. And he had known all along he would have to share some essential truths about himself with her.

He'd told himself the right time would present itself.

And he'd been correct: it had.

Spotting *The Tiphys* at sea had been not just the right but the perfect time to tell her about his father. To admit the truth of their relationship—if that was even the correct word for it.

Only then Effie had made an assumption…the wrong assumption. She had mistakenly thought that the reason he didn't share a surname with Andreas was down to some kind of noble desire on his part to strike out on his own.

She had looked up at him, those huge amber eyes filled with such wonder, and even though he'd known that it had nothing at all to do with him—that the man she was imagining didn't actually exist—he had been momentarily lost in what it would feel like to deserve that look. If he had truly been that man, instead of one with bitter resentment in his heart.

After that, there had been no way he could tell her that he hadn't chosen to be Achileas Kane. That his father had not just withheld the name of

Alexios but denied his paternity, disowned the very existence of his son.

But it wasn't just about him.

Nothing was any more, it seemed.

It was about Effie, too, and she was essentially a good person. If he told her the truth about his father's behaviour, then it would be hard not to reveal that his motives for marriage were a lot less altruistic than he was making out. And for some reason her respect, her believing him to be a good son, mattered.

Mattered more than punishing his father.

His spine stiffened. Was that true?

For longer than he could remember he had wanted to get even with Andreas. To take back what was rightfully his.

All those years he had worked sixteen, twenty hours a day, six days a week, sometimes seven, to build his empire, he had lived and breathed that goal. This engagement to Effie was supposed to be his way of making it happen. Besting his father's lie with one of his own—a better one.

Only each decision he made had some knock-on effect he hadn't considered—like some giant game of cosmic pinball. That was why he had ended up asking her to the Galanólefki Ball… to distract her, and to distract himself from the hidden truths he was keeping.

And a part of him wanted to go, wanted to

play Prince Charming to her Cinderella. To see her smile. To make her smile.

But mostly he just wanted to stay here, with her. For it to be just the two of them. He wanted to be able to reach out and touch her, to watch her eyes widen as he found the sweet spot inside her that made her body twitch as if she couldn't control it—

Gritting his teeth against the serrated edge of hunger sawing into his groin, he got to his feet and walked across the room to stand by the open French windows. Maybe he would call it off… tell her he was feeling sick.

Not tonight, Josephine, he thought, a reluctant smile pulling at the corners of his mouth—

'Achileas?'

His heart thudded against his ribs. He still hadn't got used to the way she said his name—as if it was a prayer, or a poem…a promise, even.

But as he spun round, he forgot about his name. He forgot to breathe.

Effie was standing in the doorway.

This time he had told her to choose a dress she liked. No budget. Just something that made her feel comfortable in her own skin.

A slow, crawling tension slid over him. Maybe that hadn't been such a good idea. In fact, he was beginning to think that he should have insisted on a dress that focused on his comfort.

How the hell was he going to keep his hands to himself?

Made of pleated chiffon, her dress was the same blue as the sea where it hugged the coastline. It had a high neck with some kind of ribbon tie, and an ankle-skimming hem, but in between it clung to her body like moss to a rock.

And as she moved towards him, on silver heels that added three inches to her height, he caught a glimpse of smooth, bare thigh and realised that despite its demure length there was a leg-showcasing slit in the swirling skirt.

She stopped in front of him, teetering a little on the thick rug.

He had assumed she would put her hair up. But it was loose, casual, spilling over her bare shoulders in a way that made her look young and fresh and sexy. And then there was that intoxicating but not in-your-face scent she wore, which made all five of his senses shiver at once.

It was impossible to look and not touch and, reaching out, he ran his finger along her collarbone.

'You look beautiful.' *Make that exquisite*, he thought, watching the flush of colour flare along her cheekbones. She really was his Cinderella.

She touched his lapel lightly, one of those tentative, sanity-sapping smiles pulling at her mouth. 'So do you.' Now she bit into her lip. 'I didn't keep you waiting too long, did I?'

'I'd wait all night for you.' It wasn't something he could have imagined himself doing, much less saying to any other woman, but he wanted to say it to Effie.

Her eyes met his. 'Thank you. I was just taking a few photos. To show my mum later.'

He nodded and held out his arm.

Over the last few days, they had talked about her mum, and he'd learned that before her stroke Sam had been a beautician. And even after her stroke she'd been a good mother. It was Sam who had encouraged Effie to launch her perfume business. And it was Sam who had refused to let Effie take care of her after the second stroke.

She had nothing. No partner to support her. No money. Poor health. But she wanted the best for her daughter.

His chest tightened. Somehow, he didn't think that this sham engagement would come under that heading.

Outside, the helicopter crouched like a dragonfly on a waterlily pad, and he helped Effie climb inside. Was that why he felt so on edge? He stared through the glass at the darkening sky. Possibly. Or more likely it was the thought of being on the mainland, within spitting distance of Andreas's huge fabled waterside mansion.

The old familiar ache spread through his chest like an oil spill from a crippled tanker.

A mansion he had yet to visit.

Not that his father was even there, he thought as the helicopter began its descent. At their last meeting—only the second in his life—Andreas had told him that he had a horse running in the Kentucky Derby and would be watching the race in person.

If Andreas had been coming tonight, he wouldn't even have mentioned the ball to Effie. It was too soon for her to meet the father he barely knew. And it was more than that. Once Effie met his father, their relationship would be like a ticking time bomb. All of this—the two of them together—would have to take a back seat, and he wasn't ready for that to happen just yet.

His father's absence should have calmed him, only he couldn't seem to shake his unease…this nervousness that had never troubled him before.

As the helicopter landed, he felt Effie's body tense and, glancing through the window, he saw that the red-carpeted steps to the observatory were hemmed in on either side by a phalanx of press and photographers.

Instantly he felt a rush of relief at having found an explanation for his uncharacteristic jitters. Always before he had been with a woman for whom this was the norm, but this was all new and probably terrifying for Effie, so naturally he was worrying about her.

'It's okay.' He reached for her hand. 'They can't go inside.' His fingers tightened around hers. 'And I know it looks scary but it's really quite easy. Think of it as a dance. All you have to do is stop, smile, wave and turn.'

She nodded. 'Okay.'

'Oh, and one more thing.' He pulled her closer and kissed her softly. 'Don't let go of my hand.'

Head spinning, Effie followed Achileas along the covered roped-off walkway. Beneath the tented ceiling it felt like a cocoon, but as she stepped outside white light exploded on every side of her. She flinched, blinking. She had seen people walk the red carpet on TV countless times, but she'd had no idea it was like this—so intense, so intrusive.

Don't let go of my hand.

It was the last thing Achileas said to her before the car door had opened. Not that she'd needed telling. Blinded by the camera flashes, she hardly knew which way was up, and his hand, firmly threaded through hers, was the only thing keeping her on her feet. His other hand was curved around her waist, and she let him guide her forward—and then he stopped.

Stop. Smile. Wave. Turn.

'Well done,' he whispered against her ear.

Glancing up at him, Effie felt her stomach flip over in a totally uncontrollable response. There could be no man alive more suited to the clean elegance of a classic tuxedo than Achileas Kane.

He looked stupidly handsome—as if an artist had drawn him, each mark, each line perfectly capturing every hard plane.

It had been hard to look away before. Now it was beyond her.

'Are you ready?'

She felt his gaze move over her, the blue gleam against the gold of his skin reminding her of Ancient Egyptian artefacts.

She nodded.

'Then let's go to the ball,' he said softly.

Hand in hand, they walked up a flamboyantly wide staircase, and then they were inside the huge galleried room.

Looking down, she felt her breathing jolt. There were at least twenty white-clothed tables, glittering with silverware, and milling around between them were the guests. The men in dark suits and white shirts and the women in every shade of blue from sky to sapphire and deeper still, to indigo and midnight.

And flanking them on either side of the room was a line of statues. Not of stone or marble, but of cream-coloured flowers.

She breathed in. Roses, to be precise.

The smell was intoxicating.

His hand still locked tightly with hers, Achileas led her downstairs. She had thought this would be the easy part, but outside with the cameras flashing she had been unable to see anything. Now she could see everyone—and they could see her.

But as they moved between the groups of guests she started to relax. Everyone was friendly and there was so much to enjoy and take in. And not just with her eyes. As well as the statues there were ruins created out of jasmine and gardenias, and their scent filled the room so that she felt almost drugged.

Or perhaps that was Achileas, she thought helplessly, because right now everything about him, from his precision-tooled bone structure to his teasing, tempting smile, was making her head spin.

And she was not the only one feeling that way.

All around her she could sense women shifting to look furtively over their partners' shoulders, drawn by the magnetic north of Achileas's masculine beauty.

'Let's grab a drink,' he whispered in her ear.

It was such a normal thing to say, but the drinks here were anything but. Like everything else, the cocktails were colour-coordinated to the ball, so there were white margaritas and sapphire martinis. They looked so pretty Effie could hardly bear to drink hers, and she had only taken a few sips when dinner was announced.

The food was delicious. An astonishing granita using the ingredients of a Greek salad, a pairing of white chocolate and cured fish roe, an amazing lamb and shallot *stifado*, and to finish a lemon and basil mousse with a vanilla biscuit and olive oil ice cream.

'Thank you. Dimitris,' Achileas said as the waiter deftly cleared away their plates. 'It was all wonderful. Could you pass on my compliments to the chef?'

The waiter nodded. 'Yes, sir. I'll be sure to tell him, Mr Kane.'

Effie blinked. It was the first time she had heard Achileas speak in that way—at least to someone like a waiter. Probably he was on his best behaviour because they were here at the ball. Although most of the other guests at their table were talking too loudly to notice.

'What?' He raised an eyebrow.

'Nothing.' She hesitated. 'It's just that it was nice of you. To say that to the waiter.'

'You mean Dimitris?' His glittering blue gaze moved over her face. 'I poached Yiannis from this event a couple of years back, so I thought I'd just lay down a marker. Oh, and a wise woman once told me that waiters were people too. And that they have names.'

She felt as if a hand had reached into her chest and squeezed it. He had done it for her. It wasn't a big deal, or anything, but she could feel it tingling inside her.

At some point an orchestra had arrived and discreetly set up. Now they were playing Gershwin show tunes, and maybe it was the wine and the roses, but she felt like dancing.

'Can you dance?' She looked over at Achileas. 'Or do you just stop, smile, wave and turn?'

'Of course I can dance.' He shifted back in his seat. 'Why? Are you asking me?'

The teasing gleam in his blue eyes made her heart quiver. 'Yes, I'm asking.' Her palms were itching to touch him properly. To feel his hands on her body.

'In that case, I'm dancing.'

She stood up, suddenly impatient, but he didn't lead her onto the dance floor. Instead, he steered her through the couples moving in slow circles out of the ballroom.

'I thought we were going to dance,' she protested.

'We are. But not with all those people around us. I want to be alone with you.'

He didn't mean it the way it sounded—she knew that. He was, she was sure, just relieved to have made it this far, and he was naturally better at all this stuff…especially at saying things that sounded intimate and personal.

That was the part she had skipped. Whereas Achileas was an expert—and you didn't get to be that good without putting in the hours. Something wrenched inside her at the thought of how many women that meant, how many beds, how many kisses—

'What is going on in your head?' Achileas said quietly as he pushed open a door, then closed it behind them. He was staring down at her, his eyes intent, questioning.

'Nothing. I was just trying to work out how many guests there are,' she lied. 'Only maths isn't my strong point.'

'Four hundred. But why count them when you could be counting the stars?'

He clicked his fingers and she gasped as the ceiling above their heads turned into a swirling galaxy of thousands of luminous white stars, sparkling against midnight-blue. His arms curled around her waist, and she leaned into him, staring dazedly up at the spinning night sky.

They were in the planetarium.

'It's beautiful,' she whispered, turning to face him. 'But are we allowed in here?'

He shook his head. 'Not officially, no. But I bribed Manos and Stathis, the security guards, to take a little stroll round the block.'

She laughed, breathless, dizzy with a happiness she had never felt before. 'You know their names too?'

'Absolutely. I'm also on first name terms with Aris. He's the technician. He's in charge of the lights and the audio.'

He clicked his fingers again and the sounds of the orchestra from downstairs filled the room.

'Let's dance,' Achileas said softly.

He wrapped his hand around her waist, pulling her against him, and they waltzed slowly around the room. She felt oddly fragile, and once again she wished that she had more experience. Was this how having sex made you feel about a person? Not just physically close, but as if the other person was a part of you, fused with you in a way that had nothing to do with bodies?

It must be, she concluded. That was why she was so attuned to his every movement, his every breath.

'You're full of surprises Achileas Kane,' she said, tightening her hand against the swell of his shoulder.

'Me?' He frowned. 'What about you? Every time I think I've got you pinned down you kick my legs out from under me. There are those lightning flashes of temper. And this dress...' his gaze dropped a notch '...not forgetting, of course, the body beneath the dress. And now it turns out you dance like Cyd Charisse in *Singin' in the Rain.*'

His hand pressed against her back, and he drew her closer, so that she could feel every detail of his muscular body. She knew the film. Her mum loved it. But surely, he meant Debbie Reynolds?

'I wouldn't have had you down as a fan of old musicals,' she said lightly.

Something shifted in his face, just for a moment. 'My mother loves them,' he said at last. 'I guess I watched them so many times I ended up loving them too. Although obviously that's just between you and me.'

Her heart was beating too fast. It was the first time he had mentioned his mother directly and she wanted to ask more questions, only she could sense a reluctance, a hesitation beneath his words. Then again, most sons were protective of their mothers.

'Of course.' She kept her face serious. 'What happens in the planetarium stays in the planetarium.'

He laughed then, and suddenly she couldn't stop smiling.

'As it happens,' she added, 'my mum loves old musicals too.'

'So, she was the one who taught you to dance?'

Effie shook her head. 'No, that was my dad. He was into swing and jive, you know, Lindy Hop, that kind of thing. Before everything bad happened, he used to take my mum out dancing on a Saturday night. Our neighbour Mrs Barker would come and sit with me.'

Her fingers trembled against his arm. She had forgotten those evenings—how her dad, handsome in his suit and tie, would let her stand on his shoes while he danced around the tiny flat, her mother laughing and clapping at the edge of the room.

'I'm sorry.' Achileas's face was serious now, his smile gone. 'I didn't mean to upset you—'

'You didn't. It's a nice memory. Usually, I only remember the bad things.' She bit her lip. 'Thank you.'

Beneath the glittering stars, his skin looked like polished bronze. 'You don't need to thank me.'

'But I do. I know my dad is a long way from perfect, but it's been such a long time since I've thought about him in a good way. And it was good sometimes. I think I need to remember that, because it's not a great idea to hold on to the bad. Sometimes you have to grip really tightly to the good, otherwise you get stuck in the past.'

It was probably the longest speech she had made in her life, too long maybe because they had stopped moving now and he was staring at her, breathing a little unsteadily.

'Why do you think I'm holding on to you so tightly?' he said at last. His voice was taut, like a bow before the arrow flew. 'You're a good person, Effie. Good for me. Too good for me.'

A frown pleated his forehead and he muttered something in Greek. Then he lowered his face and kissed her.

His mouth drove the breath from her. There was a white flash, brighter than all the stars above them combined. She felt him slant his head, adjusting the fit of his mouth to hers, and then he kissed her again—kissed her as though it was years, not hours, since he had last kissed her.

And she couldn't get enough. Even if it meant never taking another breath. She wanted to taste him—all of him. She wanted all of his heat and his hardness—

Her fingers bit into the swell of his biceps. 'Can we go back to the villa?'

She felt the muscles along his jaw tighten as he breathed out against her mouth and knew that he was feeling the same shattering hunger. 'Yes. I think that would be a good idea.'

He pulled her closer and she clutched at him, feeling the hardness of him through her dress, and he kissed her again—quickly this time, as though he didn't trust himself to linger.

He led her back through the building, walking so fast and with such a sense of purpose that she had to run to keep up.

'Sorry—' Slowing his pace, he turned and gave her a smile that was both apologetic and shimmering with a need that made her breath dissolve. 'I wasn't thinking of you in heels,' he said, leading her carefully down the staircase. 'Well, I was, but not in that—'

He broke off, and his grip on her arm tightened almost painfully. Glancing up at his face, she felt her breath catch. His smile hadn't so much faded as shifted into a different version of itself, like a tree shedding leaves in the autumn.

'What is it? Have you changed your mind?'

But Achileas didn't answer. Nor was he looking at her. His eyes were fixed on a grey-haired man standing at the bottom of the staircase. Standing…watching. Waiting.

Her breath died in her throat.

She had never seen him before in her life, but he was so familiar to her. Still handsome, his hair greying now, with straight, symmetrical features and those blue, blue eyes.

The same blue eyes as his son.

Her gaze moved silently between the two men, and she knew without any doubt that she was looking at Achileas's father. She knew because it was like looking through a book of fabric samples where the pattern was the same, but the colour was slightly different.

For a moment, neither man spoke nor moved. They were like two ships run aground on sandbanks.

And then finally the older man inclined his head. 'Achileas. What a pleasant surprise.'

His gaze hovered for a moment where his son's arm curved around Effie's waist, and then it lasered in on her face. She blinked. Beside her, Achileas stood stiffly in silence.

Motivated as much by good manners as panic, she held out her hand. 'Hi, I'm Effie—Effie Price. I'm…' She hesitated, unsure suddenly of how to finish the sentence she had started.

But, reaching out and taking her hand, Andreas Alexios finished it for her. 'Engaged,' he said, tilting the diamond up to the light as he kissed her fingers. 'Congratulations, my dear.' His smile was as smooth and polished as his voice. 'I'm afraid we haven't been introduced. I'm—'

'My apologies.'

With a rush of relief, Effie felt Achileas move beside her, and she turned to him, smiling. But as she looked up into his face, she felt her smile freeze. He was smiling too, but his eyes were as flat and distant as the horizon.

'Effie, this is Andreas Alexios. My father.'

'It's very nice to meet you,' Effie said carefully, trying and failing to follow the twisting undercurrents of the conversation. It was clear neither man had expected to see the other—but surely that was a cause for joy, not caution?

As if reading her mind, Andreas tilted his head again and said in the same polished voice, 'We should celebrate.' Turning slightly, he narrowed his eyes across the crowded ballroom. 'Now, where is Eugenie? Ah, there she is—'

Achileas's mother!

Curiosity overcoming her confusion, Effie followed the direction of his gaze. She felt a jab of both admiration and disappointment. Dressed in the palest blue of a dawn sky, the woman talking to a couple at the edge of the dance floor was younger than Andreas, and very beautiful, but she looked nothing like her son. Achileas was all molten heat. Eugenie Alexios was cool and blonde and regal—like a storybook snow queen.

Beside her, Andreas was making one of those small, indefinable but unmistakably autocratic gestures with his hand that had several waiters running across the room. 'I think champagne is in order,' he said softly.

'That would be—' Effie began.

'A bad idea,' Achileas interrupted. His arm tightened around her waist. 'We've had a busy few weeks and Effie is feeling a little done in. We were just on our way home when we bumped into you.'

'A pity.' Andreas frowned. 'But you should certainly go home, my dear. Get some rest. However, I insist you both join us for lunch tomorrow. After all, we have a lot to talk about.'

'Tomorrow, then,' Achileas said, and before she had a chance to say goodbye, he had caught her elbow and was propelling her through the building.

But why were they leaving? He hadn't even spoken to his mother. Nor, as it turned out, was he planning on speaking to her.

On their journey back to the villa Achileas was silent—the kind of silence that was like a heavy, stifling shroud. Her pulse trembled. She knew he was angry. She just didn't know why. Although she suspected it had something to do with his need to be in control. Each time things had come to a head between them, that had been the touchpaper for the ensuing fireworks.

But he had been so abrupt with his father, rude almost and it made her feel as if she had been rude by association. She knew she should be angry too, and she was—only every time she caught sight of his rigid profile the flame of her anger seemed to go out like too-damp kindling.

Back at the villa, the staff who had been waiting for their return took one look at Achileas's dark, dangerous expression and retreated. Effie glanced around the empty sitting room. Now it was just the two of them.

And then there was one, she thought, as he stalked through the French windows onto the balcony.

Taking a breath, she followed him. The sky was littered with stars, just as it had been in the planetarium, only these stars were joined by a huge pale moon.

Beneath it, Achileas was leaning against the rail, looking at the dark Aegean, a part of the darkness, almost. And now he reminded her not of his father, but hers. A man who had gambled big on the horses and lost. Only unless she was missing something this was what he had wanted to happen.

'Do you want to talk?' she said quietly, and

at the sound of her voice he turned, as she knew he would.

But not to talk but to blame.

'I think you've done enough talking for one night, don't you?' he snarled, his anger circling her like a narrow-eyed panther.

So, she had been right. This was about her not waiting for him to make the introductions. But for him to get so angry was not just unreasonable, it was illogical. 'He's your father, Achileas. I could hardly just ignore him.'

'But you didn't have to tell him about the engagement.'

'I didn't. He saw the ring. But why wouldn't I tell him anyway? Isn't that why we're doing this? For him?' She took a step forward, wanting to touch him, to lead him back to that place of closeness they had found. 'Look, I know it was a shock, the two of you meeting like that, and I know you probably had it all planned out in your head—'

'You don't know anything.' He walked towards her, his movements precise with fury. 'You don't know anything about me.'

She flinched from his words as if he had hit her. And she felt as if he had.

It wasn't true. She *did* know him. Or had she simply got lost in the miraculous addictive hunger that gnawed at both of them? Confused that obliterating passion with a deeper understanding of the man standing in front of her with his hands balled at his sides?

'You're right. I don't understand why this is a problem. So talk to me. Tell me what I need to know.'

'I don't need you to know anything. I don't need you.'

'Everybody needs someone,' she said, trying to stay calm, or at least sound it. 'If you can't talk to me then talk to your father. Or your mother.'

The angry creature pacing beside her stumbled, and she felt her heart twist, remembering the beautiful, elegant blonde woman at the ball who was so unlike her own mother. And yet they shared a love of old musicals…

She felt a sudden tilting vertigo, as if she had drunk the champagne Andreas had suggested. Something had occurred to her—something so shattering she could hardly believe it.

'Except she's not your mother, is she? Eugenie, I mean?' she said quietly.

He didn't move a muscle. He didn't even tense.

And yet she felt his reaction like a burst of electromagnetic energy, just as if a lightning bolt had struck him and the effects were pulsing from his body into hers.

She was right.

Achileas was staring at her. His breathing wasn't quite steady, and his eyes looked strange, the pupils huge and dark. He had looked at her like that once before, but when?

'Achileas…' she said softly.

But as she reached for him, he turned and walked away without a backward glance, and was instantly swallowed up by the darkness. And now, she really was alone.

CHAPTER TEN

STARING AFTER HIM, Effie felt short of breath as she remembered when she had seen that look on Achileas's face before. It had been back in London, in his limousine, right after she'd accused him of hiding.

And now he was hiding again. Out there in the darkness.

Her head was full of panic. She needed to go after him, find him, but he could be anywhere.

No, not just anywhere.

She felt her heartbeat slow. She knew where he was. He had gone there before, and he would go back there for the same reason. To lift that anger and frustration, the pain he carried everywhere.

The pain of watching his mother being replaced in his father's affections.

Eugenie must be Andreas's mistress. And, knowing that, she felt everything else fall into place. Achileas's frustration with the world, that near-constant simmering anger and the strange weave of tension between the two men when they'd met at the ball.

She was sure she was right, but for the moment it didn't matter. What mattered was finding Achileas.

Even with the full moon it took her fifteen minutes to reach the lagoon. Things looked different at night, and of course it didn't help that she was wearing heels, but finally she found the path down between the sand dunes.

Achileas was not swimming this time. He had taken off his jacket and was barefoot, sitting on the sand, his shoulders slumped like Atlas, his eyes fixed on the barely moving water.

'You shouldn't have come,' he said as she sat down beside him.

He didn't turn to look at her, but she didn't need to see his face. She could read his shoulders, the set of his jaw.

'That's not up to you,' she said quietly. 'Only I expect you'll have to prove that it is, and any moment now you're going to storm off into the darkness again. I can't stop you doing that, but I'm just warning you now that I'm going to follow you.'

'And why would you do that?'

His hand flexed against the sand. But he stayed sitting beside her, and all the time he was throwing angry questions at her he was here and safe.

She stared at his rigid profile. 'You'd do the same for me. You *did* the same for me.'

'That was different. You were upset.'

And you're not? she thought.

He looked up at her, as if hearing her unspoken accusation. 'No amount of talking is going to change this.'

He meant fix this, she thought. But first he had to admit what was broken.

'Maybe not,' she admitted. 'Some things can't be changed. But sometimes they don't need to be. You just need to find a way to accept them and adapt.'

'Accept and adapt?' He shook his head, his mouth twisting into a shape that scraped at her skin. 'And you think I can do that?'

There was tension in his words, and with a jolt she realised that he didn't need to go into the darkness to hide. He was hiding all the time, using his anger and impatience to deflect prying eyes from what lay beneath.

Slipping off her sandals, she nodded. 'I think you can do pretty much anything if you set your mind to it.'

There was something flickering in his eyes that she couldn't follow. 'How did you know?' he said finally. 'That Eugenie wasn't my mother?'

Remembering Eugenie's cool, regal beauty, she said quietly, 'She didn't seem like the kind of person who likes old musicals.'

'Probably not. Truthfully, though, what would I know?' There was a tightness in his voice that made it sound flat, detached, as if it belonged to another man entirely. 'I've never met her. But then up until six months ago I'd only met my father once.'

Effie stared at him in confusion. Was that a joke? Surely it must be. But one look at his face told her that he was being serious. Mute with shock, she groped in her mind for some kind of logic that would explain his words.

'I don't understand...how is that possible?'

He shifted—a miniscule squaring of his shoulders. 'My father had a one-night stand with my mother. I was the result.'

Effie tried to make her next question sound casual. 'So they were never married?'

His face was like carved stone. 'He was already married.'

Married for seven years, she thought, mentally subtracting Achileas's age from the length of Andreas's marriage to Eugenie. Her heart started to pound. She had got it back to front. His mother had been the mistress—not Eugenie.

'How did it happen?'

His hands flexed against the sand again.

'At some party. Back in the day, my mother was a model. She was young and pretty. My father was on his own in New York. It was never meant to be anything but a fling. He had a wife...

children. When my mother got pregnant, he sent some lawyers to see her. They got her to sign an NDA and he paid her off.'

His shoulders rose and fell.

'Oh, and he made her agree to keep his name off the birth certificate, which was a nice touch.'

Effie stared at him, appalled. It was a detail, but there was an efficiency about it that was breathtakingly cruel.

With an effort, she cleared her throat. 'And he never got in touch?'

Achileas shook his head. 'Never. I didn't even know who my father was until I was twelve. Whenever I asked her, my mother was always so vague I used to think he was a spy, and then out of the blue she told me I was going to boarding school in England. I didn't want to go, and we argued, and she told me that I had to go because that was what my father wanted.'

His mouth twisted. 'It was one of his demands. That and learning Greek.'

Picturing a younger Achileas, Effie felt her pulse jerk. It must have been so baffling for him, and hurtful, having to comply with the dictates of a faceless stranger who cared so little about him that he had never bothered to introduce himself.

'But you did meet him eventually?'

'When I was thirteen. It was the summer term of my first year.'

She watched the muscles tighten beneath his shirt.

'I was playing rugby in the final of an inter-school tournament. We were winning, and then at half time one of my teammates told me that a Greek billionaire was presenting the cup. Some shipping tycoon called Alexios.'

The ache in his voice echoed in the darkness.

'I knew it couldn't be a coincidence. That he was there to see me. And when we walked back onto the pitch, I couldn't stop looking for him in the crowd. Of course he wasn't there. He was being wined and dined by the head teacher. But I totally lost my concentration, and we lost the match.'

Effie swallowed. His face was tight, and she knew that he could still remember it now: the nervous anticipation of finally meeting his long-absent father, the panic that it might be a big mix-up—a different Greek billionaire called Alexios.

'We had to line up to get our runner-up medals, and when I saw him, I was shocked and excited, because we looked so alike. I knew I was right. That he must be there to see me. And I was so certain he'd say something.'

He hesitated, and now his hands were still, the knuckles white.

'Only when my name was called out, he just

handed me the medal and shook my hand. As if I was just some random boy. As if I was nothing to him.'

Achileas felt his stomach clench. Even now he didn't know how he had managed to walk away as if nothing had happened. As if his whole world hadn't just spun into the crash barrier like a jack-knifing truck.

For days afterwards he had been mute with shock, and he had felt this pain—as if something had torn inside him and wouldn't heal. Eventually he'd learned to live with it, but as the pain had dulled his rage had intensified. Rage at his mother for getting pregnant. Rage with his father for rejecting him. Rage at a world that turned a blind eye to the careless, hurtful behaviour of people who were supposed to know better.

And he'd been furious for such a long time now.

He felt Effie's fingers curl around his, her small, cool hand pulling him back, calming his heartbeat.

'And after that?' she asked.

'After that I didn't see him again until six months ago.'

It had been late—around ten. Would he have picked up the phone if he had known it was Andreas? Probably. His father was like the sun to his earth. Distant, but impossible to live without.

And he had tried—tried so hard—had spent so long trying not to care, hating Andreas. But even though he had wanted to hang up, to reject his father as Andreas had rejected him, he hadn't been able to do it.

'He called me at home in New York. Said he was in town and asked if I could come and see him. I wasn't going to. I was so angry with him. I'd been angry with him for years. But I still couldn't not go.'

'What would have been the point of not going?' Effie asked quietly. 'Not seeing him wouldn't have stopped him being your father.' Her fingers tightened around his. 'I'm guessing that's when he told you he was ill?'

Achileas nodded slowly. 'He has prostate cancer, and now it's spread. He's been fighting it for years and I don't think there's much else they can do. So, he wants to set his affairs in order.'

The ache in his chest had spread to his limbs. They felt heavy and immobile. His hand in Effie's was a dead weight.

'He has three daughters, but they have nothing to do with his business, and anyway he wants his empire—his legacy—to pass down the male line.' He couldn't keep the bitterness from his voice. 'Basically, that's why he got in touch. To let me know that he was ready to acknowledge me as his son and heir, but—'

He didn't want to admit the next part—to acknowledge that his father's acceptance came with a condition attached. That for him, entry into the fabled Alexios clan came with strings.

And maybe he didn't have to. He had already admitted so much—too much. Only the effort of hiding the truth was suddenly exhausting.

Glancing over at Effie's small oval face, he felt a mix of impatience and admiration. She wouldn't give up. She would sit and wait, or if necessary, follow him to the ends of the island— probably to the ends of the earth.

'But you had to get married?' she said quietly.

His eyes found hers. They were brown beneath the moonlight, but he could still see the flecks of gold in the irises. 'Yes. And I know you must hate me—'

She stared at him. 'Why would I hate you?'

'Because I lied to you.'

'Yes, you did—for the same reason I lied to you. Because we didn't know each other, and the truth is hard for us to share with anyone, let alone a stranger.'

She spoke in that soft, precise way of hers that he found so soothing. Only he didn't want to be soothed; he didn't deserve to be.

'But I kept lying to you even after I knew how badly you'd been hurt by your father's lies. I let you think I was doing a good thing. That I was a good person—'

She frowned. 'You *are* a good person.'

'Why? Because of this? Us?'

'Yes.' The word echoed around the silent beach as she nodded. 'You're marrying someone you don't love for someone you do.'

Something wrenched inside him, and he pulled his hand free of hers and got to his feet, backing away from her as she stood up too.

'No, you're wrong. I don't love my father. I *hate* him for what he did to me—what he's still doing to me.'

The old familiar anger was rushing over him like a dark storm surge, and it was both a relief and an agony. 'I'm sorry to disappoint you, Effie, but I'm not faking this marriage to make him happy. I'm doing it to get even.'

There it was. The truth, the whole truth and nothing but the truth.

And it felt good to admit it finally.

It had been a long journey. In the beginning there had been only pain, and then afterwards that all-consuming rage. He'd understood that his father's rejection was the cause of it, but understanding hadn't eased the pain or calmed his fury. He'd known he needed to do more—needed to find some way to balance the equation or feel that way for ever.

And then suddenly the solution had been there. And the best part was that it had been his father who had inadvertently presented it to him.

'I'm going to take away his name. Do to him

what he did to me. I'm not giving him heirs. The Alexios name, and his legacy, will die with him.'

It had to. Because he had no idea how to be a father.

Effie was staring at him as if she didn't know him. For a moment he felt like a stranger to himself, but of course it was strange, finally saying out loud what he'd been thinking privately for years.

'And that's what you want?' she asked.

He nodded. 'It's what I've wanted ever since he handed me that runner-up medal.'

There was a long silence that stretched out into the darkness, and then her eyes found his and she said quietly, 'I don't believe you.'

Around them the air seemed to tremble at her words. As if a storm was approaching. Only the sky above was clear and cloudless.

'You think I'm lying? After everything I just told you.'

There was another silence, and then she took a step forward. In the moonlight her face was as pale and serious as it had been that first day outside the Stanmore, when she'd told him he should apologise to her.

'Yes, I do. But only because you're having to lie to yourself. Look, we both know patience isn't one of your virtues, Achileas. If you really wanted to punish your father as badly as you say, then you would have been desperate to get on with it. As soon as you saw Andreas you would have told him about the engagement. But you did the opposite—'

'It wasn't the right time.'

'Of course it wasn't.'

Her voice was gentle—too gentle—and something inside him…something that had always been hard and impermeable…started to crumble.

'It's never going to be the right time. Because you don't hate your father and you don't want to punish him. You love him and you want to get to know him.'

His heart was a dark weight in his chest as he felt her hand touch his.

'He reached out to you.'

Taking a breath, he forced himself to speak. 'I'm just a means to an end for him.'

'Maybe.' She was silent for a moment. Then, 'Or maybe he needed a reason to reach out. He's old and ill, but he's also proud. He made some choices when he was younger than you—wrong choices—and maybe forcing this marriage on you is his way of trying to right those wrongs without losing face.'

She stroked his cheek with her fingertips.

'I don't know for sure, but I think you have more in common with Andreas than just your looks.'

She was so certain of the goodness of his motives, so certain that there was good in the world.

He envied that belief and he wanted to prove her right.

But she was wrong.

Wrong about the world.

Wrong about him.

'You're right.' Watching her face soften, he hated himself for what he was about to say, but he couldn't pretend—not to Effie…not now. 'Andreas and I gave up on each other a long time ago. Me marrying you can't change that, and it won't. You see, I can't forgive him, and I don't love him. I don't know how to love, and I don't want to know.'

He couldn't put himself in the position of needing someone. Couldn't risk yet more rejection, more pain.

'I'm not like your father,' he said. 'I can't gamble my happiness on someone else's throw of the dice. And I know that's not what you want to hear but I don't want to lie to you. Not now. Not anymore.'

In the moonlight, her eyes were like polished amber stones, vivid like flames against her flushed cheeks. He leaned forward and kissed her softly, feeling his own body flame in response. But as he moved to deepen the kiss her hands pressed against his chest and she backed out of his arms.

'Effie…?'

He watched her turn and walk slowly towards

the water, and then she reached around and undid the ribbon around her throat. His heart missed a beat as the blue chiffon fluttered down her body onto the sand.

His gaze sharpened.

She was completely naked, her head to one side as she gazed down at the tiny waves rippling over her feet. He swallowed, dry-mouthed. Silhouetted against the moonlight, her body was the single most erotic sight he'd ever seen.

'What are you doing?' he said hoarsely.

She didn't look back at him. 'I'm going for a swim.'

Now she was in the water.

Frowning, he took a step forward. 'But you told me you couldn't swim.'

The water was up to her shoulders. 'I can't. But that doesn't change the fact that I'm here... going for a swim.'

He was already running into the waves as she disappeared beneath the surface, and then suddenly she was in his arms, her hair slick against her head, her eyelashes splayed like starfishes.

Swearing loudly, he hauled her against him. 'What the hell are you playing at?'

Her hands gripped his shoulders and her beautiful eyes locked onto his. 'I just wanted to prove to you that when things can't be changed, you can accept them and adapt.'

'By drowning?'

She bit into her lip. 'I wasn't drowning. I was waving, so you knew where to find me.'

'I know where to find you, Effie. You're by my side.'

The truth in those words tore him in two. He had imagined a woman who would be able to fake a marriage with him, but Effie was so much more than that. She would risk her life for him. Only what about now? Now that she knew the truth?

He might not know about love, but he knew Effie. He knew how much it hurt her to lie, and that she had only done so because she'd thought his motives were good. Something twisted inside him. If this arrangement was going to continue it would have to be her choice.

'But maybe that needs to change,' he said slowly. 'Because I can't. I can't adapt or accept what Andreas did to me. To my mother. I need to do this. I need to win.'

His need for revenge was like a living, breathing shadow—always at his heels, night, and day. And nothing could change that.

There was no sound except their breathing. Around them the universe was silent, as if shocked by his words.

'I know that's how you feel.'

Her face was pale, but her voice was grave and certain, and he felt a rush of relief that he hadn't managed to push her away like everyone else.

'I know why you feel that way. And that's enough for me. Nothing's changed.'

'You still want to do this?' He'd been so scared she would quietly refuse to go any further.

For a moment she didn't reply and then her eyes found his. 'We still have a deal, don't we?'

The sudden reminder of the reason Effie was there was like a physical blow. But he knew it was irrational to feel that sting beneath his ribs.

He nodded. 'Yes, we do, but—'

'Okay, then.'

Glancing down, he caught sight of her bare breasts and their rosy-tipped nipples. Instantly the sting beneath his ribs was forgotten as heat rushed through him.

'How did you know where to find me?' he asked.

Her lashes flickered up. 'I saw you the other morning…swimming.' A pulse began to beat wildly in her throat. 'You were naked.'

There was a moment of sharpening silence and then he drew her against him, his body tensing as he felt her bare, wet skin slide over his soaked clothes.

'And now you are,' he said softly.

Their eyes locked for a full sixty seconds and then he jerked her against him, taking her mouth as if he owned it, parting her lips and kissing her hungrily. She moaned softly, curling her hands around his neck, wrapping her legs around his waist, and he lifted her again, pushing forward through the water.

Reaching the sand, he laid her down, kissing her high on her neck, then low on her jawbone, feeling her body shudder.

'Wait a minute.'

He leaned back and wrestled his soaked shirt up and over his head. Keeping his eyes trained on her face, he yanked his trousers open, his jaw clenching as she freed him from the wet fabric of his boxers.

He was already so hard...

Sucking in a breath, Effie wrapped her hand around his smooth, straining erection, her nipples tightening painfully as Achileas lowered his mouth to her breast and licked first one and then the other.

His hand was moving between her thighs, parting her to the cool night air and she moved against his hand, arching her back away from the wet sand, lifting her body, maddened by his touch, needing more of him. Her pulse accelerated as she felt the hard length of him dig into her stomach. So close to the soft, slick heat between her thighs.

But not close enough.

Grabbing his hips, she pulled him closer, and he grunted, grabbing himself, sucking in a breath.

'I haven't got a condom, Effie.'

Her stomach clenched. She stared at him in shock. She hadn't thought this through. But then she hadn't been thinking at all—or at least not in any logical way.

Her head had been spinning from everything Achileas had told her, and she'd been fighting the weight of his anger and pain. Her pain, too, for failing to help him—just as she had failed to help her father with his demons. But then he'd kissed her, and she had kissed him back, and that had been unthinking too...instinctive.

Necessary.

Only she had forgotten about protection.

'I'm due my period any day, so I should be safe...' her hands stilled against his chest '...but maybe we should go back to the villa.'

The risk of pregnancy was almost non-existent. But she had heard the tension in his voice when he had spoken about not giving his father heirs.

'No.' The muscles in his face were tight. 'I want you now.'

'I want you too,' she said hoarsely.

He rolled over, taking her with him so that she was straddling his hips, and she shivered inside and out as his hands caught her by the waist and he lifted her, sliding the blunt head of his erection against her clitoris back and forth, until she thought she would die from pleasure.

She leaned forward, pressing her forehead into his, and now he pushed inside her, thrusting deeply and then withdrawing to thrust again, in a hard, intoxicating rhythm that made her moan against his mouth. It was coming. She could feel her body starting to fray around him, unravelling faster and faster, in time with his hips.

And then her muscles tensed, and she was shuddering against him, feeling his stubble rasping against her cheek as he lunged forward and his body spilled forcefully into hers.

CHAPTER ELEVEN

LEANING BACK AGAINST the leather banquette seat, Achileas stared across the blue water, his heart pounding in time with the thump of the launch's hull as it bounced over the waves. It was finally happening. Today, for the first time, he was going to step inside the Villa Thymári— Andreas's waterside mansion.

In his head it had become a mythical place. A kind of Greek Camelot.

His shoulders tensed.

Guinevere's failure to produce an heir had, in part, led to the fall of King Arthur's legendary home. Did he still want that to happen to the house of Alexios?

He had thought so. In all the years he'd spent plotting his revenge, it had been the yin to the yang of Andreas's rejection. The ultimate sting in the tail.

But if that was the case, why had he had unprotected sex with Effie on the beach?

Short answer: because he hadn't wanted to wait.

Long answer…

He frowned. Was there a long answer? Basically, he had wanted her, there and then, and she had seemed certain it was safe, and he had trusted her.

His eyes shifted to the woman sitting beside him as he tested that sentence inside his head. It was true: he did trust Effie. But it had still been a stupid risk to take. He didn't want children. He didn't have the right instincts. How could a fatherless boy be a father?

And yet he couldn't seem to get the idea out of his head that she could be pregnant. That a baby…their baby…might be forming inside her.

And for some reason it wasn't freaking him out.

There was a reason, he told himself firmly. He'd waited so long to get even with his father and now the moment of reckoning was finally here, so naturally he was feeling completely off-balance.

His chest tightened. It wasn't just that.

When Effie had told him that he loved his father and wanted to get to know him, not punish him, it had been as if she had thrown a light switch and spun him round in the darkness. And now he didn't know up from down.

She was wrong, but it had knocked him off course like a rogue wave, sweeping away all the recognisable pointers.

Not all of them, he thought, gazing at the woman sitting beside him. Effie had made her way to him in the darkness. And remembering the moment when she'd sat down beside him on the sand, he felt calm again—safe, like a ship in a storm seeing the beam of a lighthouse marking out a safe path through the rocks ahead.

On impulse he caught her arm, turning her and pulling her against him.

'We haven't really talked about what happened last night. I know you said you thought it was safe, but I want you to know that you don't need to worry,' he said quietly. 'I'll look after you. I mean, if you are—'

'I won't be,' she said quickly. She smiled stiffly. 'My period is due in a day or two, so I'm completely safe.'

Safe in that she almost certainly wasn't pregnant, Effie thought as his eyes locked with hers. But she wasn't safe from the hunger in his narrowed blue gaze, or the softness of his mouth, or the hard, insistent press of his body...

Wasn't that why they were having this conversation? Because he made her reckless? Made her want things...need things? Made her lose control. Made her walk into the sea even though she could barely swim.

His touch made her shiver inside—made her

feel so hollowed out with longing there was nothing else. Certainly no common sense.

What other explanation could there be for what she had let happen—no, conspired to make happen? Sex without protection was beyond reckless—it was crazy.

What if it hadn't been that time of the month? Would she still have taken the risk? It was one thing lying to other people, but they couldn't lie about their relationship to a child. A child Achileas didn't want. And yet he had been as reckless as her.

Stomach cartwheeling, she stared ahead to where a huge, pale house sat like an opal on a ring beside the shimmering aquamarine water. Why would he take a risk like that?

Of course the answer to that was obvious. Clearly his head had been all over the place. But in time, with her support, that could change—

In time? With her support?

She wasn't safe from that either. That instinct, inherited straight from her mother, to hope for the best, to go with the flow however bad things were, however painful it was for her to do so, and wait for things to change.

Last night all of the above had crowded in on her, and that was why she had walked into the water, then had unprotected sex with a man who didn't want children.

But it wouldn't happen again.

There would be no further risk-taking.

What had happened last night had been a one-off. Everything had been so raw, so painful, and sex had been both a balm, and a place to get lost. A place to hide from the swirl of emotions churning inside her. Pushing aside all those confusing and confused feelings, she had chosen to embrace her need and his—because it had been all either of them could handle.

That was their truth. That dark, mesmerising hunger. That shimmering fire.

Achileas hadn't been ready to accept the other truth. That he loved his father. Andreas's rejection still hurt him too much.

She gritted her teeth. She was doing it again. But this wasn't her problem to fix. She wasn't going to be like her mother, clinging on to something that would break her. She wouldn't and she couldn't be that woman.

That wasn't what she'd signed up for, and from now on she was going to stick to the script.

As the launch came to a stop Achileas helped her disembark, and she gazed up at Andreas's villa. It was more like a palace, really, and Achileas was like the prodigal son, returning home to sit at his father's table.

Albeit with conditions attached.

Her stomach clenched. It still shocked her that Andreas could have treated his child so ruthlessly and was manipulating him even now. Yet she was sure that there was more to it. Sure that Andreas was too proud to admit to his mistake, much less apologise for it, and that this was his way of making amends without losing face.

Not your problem, she told herself firmly as a uniformed maid stepped forward, smiling stiffly.

'Welcome to the Villa Thymári. Please, if you would follow me?'

'Thank you,' Achileas said beside her.

'Yes, thank you,' Effie added quickly.

It was stupid, but the maid's black dress and white apron felt like an omen. A reminder of that version of herself she had left behind in London.

Or she had thought she'd left behind.

The interior of the house was stunning. Walking through it, Effie felt less like Cinderella and more like the Little Match Girl. With a mix of statuary and modern art adding texture and colour to its soaring high-ceilinged rooms, the villa was cool and pale and exquisitely beautiful.

A lot like their hostess, Effie thought as Eugenie rose to greet them.

'How lovely to meet you,' she said quietly. 'Andreas has been so excited about you coming.'

If Andreas was excited, he hid it well. But perhaps if you belonged to the exclusive top one percent of the richest men in the world there was very little left to excite you. He greeted both her and Achileas in that same polished marble voice, his blue eyes moving over them like a searchlight.

'Are you recovered, Ms Price?'

'Yes, thank you, Kýrios Alexios,' she said carefully. 'But please call me Effie.'

He inclined his head. 'And you shall call me Andreas. Now, Effie, shall we have that glass of champagne? And then we can eat.'

As she'd expected, the meal was delicious. A sea urchin and artichoke salad, followed by roasted lamb that fell off the bone and aubergine with a feta crust. To finish there was traditional Greek *kadaifi* and pink peppercorn ice cream.

The conversation was just as sophisticated. They discussed the ball, Greek political issues, and their English and American counterparts, and then Andreas and Achileas talked about something called long short equity.

Andreas seemed perfectly at ease, as if having lunch with his estranged son was something that happened every day. But although Achileas might look handsome and relaxed too, with his hand curving easily around the stem of his wine glass, there was a taut set to his body—as if he was holding a kite steady in a high wind.

And that was understandable. He was in his father's home. Finally. She could only try to imagine what that would feel like to the boy who had been handed a runner-up medal by the same man over two decades ago.

A man who had silver-framed photos of three beautiful blonde women prominently displayed on every surface. Three sisters. His daughters. Achileas's half-sisters.

Their mother, Eugenie, was also on edge. Outwardly the older woman was the perfect smiling hostess, polite and attentive to their every need. Occasionally, though, her serene smile seemed to slip a little, as if it was an effort to keep it in place.

Not that Effie could blame her. How must it feel to be confronted by living proof of your husband's infidelity and betrayal? Had she known what Andreas had done at the time? Did she know what he was doing now?

It was impossible to tell. It was as if she was trapped beneath glass.

After dessert, they moved outside. Eugenie had been called away to the phone, so it was just the three of them sitting on the wide leather sofas beneath a huge white canopy.

'Your coffee, Ms Price.'

'Thank you.' Effie smiled up at the maid—different maid, same uniform—feeling again that twinge of unease.

'Achileas tells me you were in the hospitality sector before you decided to set up your own business.' Andreas leaned back, his blue eyes moving with deceptive carelessness over Effie's face. 'Working as a chambermaid.'

'Yes, I was. I worked at the Stanmore in London,' she said, lifting her chin. 'I would have liked to concentrate on my perfumery sooner, but I needed to work to pay the rent.'

Andreas nodded. 'Everyone has to start somewhere. And you were working at the hotel when you met my son?'

'She was.' Achileas leaned forward and picked up his coffee cup, positioning himself between her and his father. 'But she wasn't at work when we met again and got to know one another.' He turned, his blue eyes resting on her face, his gaze fierce and unwavering. 'That was later.'

Her chest tightened—no, that was wrong. It felt more as if it was being stretched...stretched almost to its limits...by something building inside her that she couldn't name.

There was a beat of silence and Andreas smiled. 'Achileas... I left some paperwork on the desk in my study for you to read through. I wonder if you might take a look.' He glanced over his shoulder and instantly the maid reappeared. 'Show Mr Kane to my office.'

Watching Achileas leave, Effie felt her heart start to beat faster. She had thought this meeting today would be an opportunity for father and son to talk. Now, though, it appeared that Andreas wanted to speak to her.

But to what end?

Still smiling, Andreas got to his feet. 'If I may,

Effie, I'd like to show you the rose garden. I think you would enjoy it. We have both the Turkish and the Damascene varieties which I believe are used extensively in perfumery.'

Naturally, she agreed, and the garden was beautiful. Arranged in a spiral, like the shell of a snail, the roses at the centre were the oldest and rarest. The smell was extraordinary—as delicate as fine wine with notes of sweet apricot, green apple and honey. It was hard not to simply stand and breathe.

Andreas seemed pleased by her reaction. 'So, has perfumery always been a passion of yours?'

Effie nodded. 'Always. My mother was a beautician, and she encouraged me when I was very little to make potions and perfumes. My idea for the business grew out of that. Although it's still at a very early stage,' she admitted.

'That might be a good thing.' The older man's eyes moved past her to the beautiful house. 'Being an Alexios comes, if you'll excuse the pun, at a *price*. Clearly there are huge benefits and privileges. Less obviously, sacrifices have to be made.'

She cleared her throat. 'What kind of sacrifices?'

'This family is a job in its own right. We are patrons of charitable foundations. We endorse political candidates. We fund and support the arts and scientific research. On top of all that, you would have a home to run—this home in the future.' He paused. 'And, of course, a family to raise.'

Remembering that moment on the beach, she felt her pulse stumble.

'I think it might be a little early to be talking about having a family.' She smiled stiffly. 'We're not even married yet.'

'But you will talk about it, I hope?'

She stared at Andreas, startled. Not by his desire for grandchildren—many parents felt the same way, her mum among them. But because Andreas had disowned his son before he was even born.

'Wouldn't it be better to wait a little?' she said carefully. 'I mean, you and Achileas have only just met. You might like some time to get to know one another.'

Andreas smiled, and there was something tyrannical about his smile. A Zeus-like disregard for the wishes of lesser mortals—even those related to him.

'Achileas understands. He knows the importance of legacy to a family like ours. I've explained to him that the name Alexios is a privilege to hand from father to son, and from son to grandson,' Andreas continued smoothly.

Father to son…son to grandson. It sounded like a prayer, and she felt a wave of pity for the old man sitting opposite her. He had lived his life always one step ahead of the pack, but he was slowing down now, and it must be hard for him to know that at some point he would stop.

But Achileas had lost so many years with him already. He needed this time with his father even if he didn't know it himself.

'I can see why you would think that, but I disagree,' she said.

Andreas frowned, and he looked so much like his son that her breathing momentarily lost its rhythm.

'I'm not sure I understand, Effie.'

'The word "privilege" makes it sound as if you have to deserve the name in some way. But I think a name is something you live up to. And on that basis, you don't need anything more from your son,' she said, her voice catching as she pictured Achileas's taut, arrogant face because his was an arrogance that masked the hurt that had shaped his character, his life. 'You should just be proud of the man he is. He's a strong man. A good man. And I—'

Her blood was pounding through her veins like the music had last night. The scent of the roses was making her feel dizzy. Except it wasn't the roses. It was something else entirely. Something that made her feel as if the garden was a boat adrift at sea. She could feel herself filling with a warm golden light, brighter than the sun, deeper than the sea, and it was in that moment, staring into Andreas's blue eyes, that she realised she was in love with his son.

But of course she was. It seemed so obvious now. Love was the reason she had followed him into the darkness last night. And the reason why she had opened her body to his without barriers. She had wanted him to know that her love was different. That it came without conditions to meet or hurdles to cross. That it was fierce and partisan and limitless.

Steadying her breathing, she said quietly, 'Achileas has worked hard his whole life to build a business of his own. He didn't need the Alexios name. What I'm trying to say is that he doesn't need your name now.'

The air seemed to still.

'In your opinion.'

Andreas's voice didn't alter, but she saw his jaw tighten.

'I'm not sure Achileas feels the same way.'

Effie stared at him, a spark of anger flaring inside her as she remembered Achileas's face in the moonlight. 'You don't know what he feels. You hardly know him.'

Andreas's blue eyes—Achileas's eyes—moved to rest on hers. 'Of course I know him. He's my son. My flesh and blood.'

Behind him, the breeze was lifting rose petals and sending them into the sky like confetti. She shook her head. 'No, that's not enough.'

Now Andreas's face was flat with shock and an anger of his own. 'Not enough? My dear, it's an unbreakable bond.'

'It should be—yes,' she agreed. 'But you broke that bond. You didn't give him a chance to be your son. You erased yourself from his life and you hurt him. You're still hurting him now...putting conditions on your acceptance.'

She felt tears burn in her eyes.

'He would do anything for you because he loves you. And I would do anything for him. I'd have any number of children with him if that was what he wanted, because I love him.'

The words left her mouth before she could check them, but she barely noticed. All that mattered was making Andreas understand what Achileas needed.

'But we won't be having a child any time soon. Not until you put him first and become a father to your son.'

'Effie—'

She spun round. Achileas was standing in the sunlight, staring at her. She pressed her hand against her forehead. How long had he been there? How much had he heard?

He was still staring at her, his eyes fixed on hers. His face was unreadable, but she could feel his anger, and his shock. Breathing shakily, she watched his gaze shift to his father, and then he was walking towards her, and her pulse slammed into her skin as his hand caught her elbow, his grip firm, precise, impersonal.

'I think I should get you home.'

Up close, she could see the tension in every line of the body she knew better than her own, and memories of that day in London tumbled through her head. Only that had been the beginning, and this felt like the end.

'Achileas...' she whispered.

But he ignored her, turning again to his father. 'Please thank Eugenie for a wonderful lunch.'

Still holding her arm, he guided her away from the house, moving swiftly and silently. She wanted to speak, to apologise, to tell him that she loved him. But the words kept slipping away like rose petals in the wind.

They reached the launch and he helped her on board.

Her heart jolted. He had stepped back onto the jetty. 'What are you doing? Aren't you coming with me?'

His face was shuttered. 'I have to talk to my father.'

'Then let me come with you—'

He cut her off. 'I don't need you to come with me.'

'I know, but I want to apologise—and I want to be there for you.'

Her stomach lurched as he shook his head slowly.

'I don't want you there.' His voice was clipped, harsh. Irrevocably final. 'Go back to the villa. I'll see you when I see you.'

'But I love you…' It was all she could force past the lump in her throat.

He stared at her in silence. 'I know,' he said finally, and then the launch started to move, and he was turning and walking back to the huge white house.

CHAPTER TWELVE

IT WAS EXACTLY the same as before, Effie thought dully as the launch bumped lightly over the waves. Except the last time Achileas had bundled her into a waiting vehicle he'd got in beside her. This time she was alone.

Back on the island, she made her way to the villa. Every step, every breath was an effort. Finally, she reached her bedroom and collapsed on the bed. She felt numb—almost as if she was floating outside of her body, watching herself.

If only that were true; then she might not have made such a mess of everything...

Her breath caught in her throat as she thought back to how she had wished for more experience. Now she had it. From a declaration of love to heartbreak in ninety seconds. Even though she had warned herself to stay detached. Told herself not to get involved.

But logic and sense were no match for love.

Love was blind, unthinking.

And in her case unrequited.

His lack of love for her was as obvious and undeniable as her love for him. And it didn't matter that they shared this exquisite bewitching chemistry. Sex wasn't love. It was a part of it, but love was about so much more than bodies moving in harmony.

It was about more than *'I'll see you when I see you.'*

A pain such as she had never felt before, that surely didn't have a name, clawed at her insides, and she got to her feet and stumbled onto the balcony. Outside the sun was softening and she breathed in deeply, the salt-scented air calming her as it had that first day.

The first day...

She could still remember that mix of panic and exhilaration as she had stood looking out across the Aegean. Everything had been ahead of her then—a future filled with possibilities. And for the first time in her life, she had been a part of those endless variables, doing more than just conjuring up adventure in a bottle.

She was living it, sharing it with Achileas. Except she wasn't. Not then, not now, not ever.

Her hands gripped the rail. Was that what it had felt like to her father? That yearning, unshakeable conviction that you were different... that the odds didn't apply to you. She had seen it so many times with Bill—the same trajectory of fervent, unquestioning belief, the euphoria as his horse nosed ahead of its rivals, and then the stunned disbelief as it lost.

She had never expected to feel that way herself. She'd always thought she was like her mum, and she had got dangerously close to following in Sam's footsteps, but she wasn't going to make the mistakes that Sam had made with her father, caring for a man who lied to himself his whole life.

And Achileas was lying. She knew he wanted, *needed* Andreas's love, but she wasn't going to wait and watch the lies he was telling himself destroy him. *And her.*

The ring on her finger caught the sun, sending a rainbow of dancing light across the pale stone. Reaching down, she tried to pull it off. She might as well get used to not wearing it.

But the ring wouldn't budge.

It was too much.

Emotion choked her, and she covered her mouth with her hand and gave in to the tears she'd been holding back ever since Achileas had walked away from the jetty.

But she couldn't cry for ever.

Two hours later, she splashed her face with cold water and stared at her reflection. She had never loved anyone before, but she knew she would never love again as she loved Achileas. There was no other man like him.

Her mouth trembled. Just thinking that made her legs buckle, but even though she had lost him she still had a life to live. It would be less of a life in so many ways, but she had her mum, and her friends, and thanks to Achileas's investment she would have the chance to make her dream of creating her own perfume brand come true.

She wasn't going to take all the money. Just the amount the bank would have given her if she had made that meeting and got the loan. Obviously, she would leave the ring behind too. Soap would get it off...

She turned towards the bathroom.

Her heart stopped.

Achileas was standing in the doorway, his blue eyes still, his face taut in the hazy light.

'Are you okay?'

The tightness in his voice made her hands ball into fists. She wanted to reach out and touch him, but he wasn't hers to touch any more. He never had been.

'I'm fine.' She forced herself to keep looking at him, even though it hurt to do so. 'Are *you* okay?'

He nodded, his eyes moving past her to the suitcase on the bed. 'You're packing.'

Not a question, a statement. In other words, he wasn't going to try and talk her out of leaving.

She nodded. 'I'm sorry, but I think it's for the best.'

'You're reneging on our deal?' He walked towards her, moving with that devastating masculine grace that made her unravel inside. 'I'm not sure you want to do that. You see, there are consequences. But perhaps you didn't read the small print?'

She had seen him angry many times before, but this felt like an entirely different emotion. She could feel it rolling off him in waves, so that it made her feel unsteady on her feet. But he could threaten what he liked. She had nothing to lose.

'I didn't. But it doesn't matter. I can't do this. I won't do this. I'm sorry if that is difficult for you to accept.'

His eyes locked on hers. 'I don't accept it.'

She wrapped her arms around her body, trying to hold in the pain that was threatening to capsize her. 'You're not being reasonable.'

'I guess not,' he agreed. 'Then again, I'm not a reasonable man. I'm selfish and arrogant and impatient. For most of my life I've been angry. And unhappy.'

Achileas tilted his dark head backwards.

'More than unhappy. I felt cursed—and then I walked into you outside the Stanmore, and everything changed. Only I didn't realise. I just kept telling myself the same lies about why I needed a wife. Why I needed you to be my wife. I told myself that I was doing you a favour.'

'You were,' she said quietly.

He wanted to laugh then—because it was laughable, ludicrous.

'No, I really wasn't. All I did was give you money, and I have so much money I could give half of it away without noticing. But you changed me. You made me look at the world in a different way.'

Watching Effie's eyes fill with tears, he felt as if his heart would burst.

'Only I didn't realise that either. I kept clinging to the past, holding on to the hate. Because I'm not just selfish and arrogant and impatient, I'm stupid too. So when you told me that I didn't want to punish my father, that I loved him, I didn't listen.' His mouth twisted. 'But the truth is, Effie, that you were right.'

She had seen beneath his anger. Seen the need to love and be loved that he had struggled against all his life.

He thought back to when he'd walked into the Alexios house. It had been the moment he had waited for all his life, and he had expected it to be transformative…seismic.

Instead, he'd felt sad, and oddly worried about the man he had hated for so long. A proud, stubborn man who was growing older and frailer. A man so much like himself.

And in that moment, he had known that some things couldn't be changed, that he needed to find a way to accept them. That it was time to accept that he wanted more than the Alexios name.

He took a step forward. 'You made me see that I had a choice. I could do what I planned—take revenge and stay angry—or I could accept that my father had already been punished enough by the stupid, selfish decision he made more than three decades ago. Only I had to do it on my own.'

Walking away from her had been the hardest thing he had ever done. Harder and more painful than walking away from Andreas at that rugby match all those years ago.

'It had to be just me and him. Can you forgive me?'

She shook her head. 'I don't need to forgive you for reaching out to your father.'

'But I hurt you.' Heart clenching, he reached out and touched her face...her sweet, serious face. 'And I'm sorrier for that than you can imagine. But if you won't let me apologise then at least let me thank you.'

'For what?'

'For everything. You made me look at myself and see who I really was beneath the suits and the stubble. Who I wanted to be. You lifted the curse. You're such a good person, Effie.'

Her lip wobbled. 'Not in the garden, I wasn't. I was rude and cruel. He's an old man, and he's sick, and he wants his family around him.'

Achileas brushed away the tears that were spilling from her beautiful amber eyes.

'He has his family. He has two sisters, and he has Eugenie and three daughters. And he has me.'

She breathed out shakily. 'So you made it all right with him?'

He shook his head slowly. 'Actually, no. I told him that you and I weren't real. That I'd set the whole marriage up because I wanted to punish him.'

Her eyes widened with such horror that he started to laugh.

'And then I told him that I didn't want or need what he was offering. That I knew what love was and that it didn't come with conditions.'

He pulled her against him, wrapping his arms around her waist, holding her close.

'It's okay. He was shocked and angry at first. You were right about us having more in common than just looks. He's got a pretty impressive temper. But then…then he apologised.'

Remembering Andreas's face, the sudden softening in his voice, Achileas heard his own voice falter. 'He said that he has regretted what he did every day. And that whatever it took, he wanted me in his life for the rest of it.'

'I'm so pleased for you.' Effie's eyes filled with tears again.

'Yeah…seems you were right about that too.

I guess in the future I'm just going to assume you're always right. It'll be easier that way.'

'The future?'

Effie felt her heart skip a beat as Achileas framed her face with his hands, forcing her to look at him.

'What you said to my father... Did you mean it? About loving me?'

There was nowhere to hide from his deep blue gaze. But she didn't want to hide ever again. Instead, she dived right in. 'Yes. Every word. I love you.'

'And I love you—'

His voice cracked as he struggled to speak, and now her heart was in freefall.

'And I know you said that you didn't think it was very likely, but if there is a baby, I'll love him or her too. I'll love every baby we have, Effie.'

'Every baby?' Her hands gripped the front of his shirt, tears of happiness and joy spilling from her eyes. 'Shouldn't we get married first?'

'Yeah, about that...'

His mouth curved into one of those smiles that made her blood turn to air.

'I know I asked you to marry me before, but I want... I need to ask you again. Will you be my wife for real, my sweet Effie...my darling Josephine?'

Searching his eyes, she saw a man in love. A

man wanting to love and be loved. She saw that the hardness, the anger, was gone.

'Effie?' he prompted, frowning, and she started to laugh. The impatience hadn't gone though.

'Yes,' she said quietly. 'Yes, I will.'

And, reaching up, she kissed him—softly at first, and then more hungrily—and he kissed her back, his arms tightening around her, holding her close with all his strength and all his passion.

* * * * *

If you got lost in the passion of
Maid for the Greek's Ring
*you're sure to love these other
Louise Fuller stories!*

**The Man She Should Have Married
Italian's Scandalous Marriage Plan
Beauty in the Billionaire's Bed
The Christmas She Married the Playboy
The Italian's Runaway Cinderella**

Available now!